THE EXECUTOR

by the same author

Silver City Scandal
The Reward Game
The Revenge Game
Fair Game
The Game
Cousin Once Removed
Sauce for the Pigeon
Pursuit of Arms

GERALD HAMMOND

THE EXECUTOR

St. Martin's Press
New York

THE EXECUTOR. Copyright © 1986 by Gerald Hammond. All rights reserved. Printed in the United States of America. No part of this book may be used or reproduced in any manner whatsoever without written permission except in the case of brief quotations embodied in critical articles or reviews. For information, address St. Martin's Press, 175 Fifth Avenue, New York, N.Y. 10010.

Library of Congress Cataloging-in-Publication Data

Hammond, Gerald.
  The executor.

  I. Title.
PR6058.A55456E9 1987   823'.914   87-4400
ISBN 0-312-00593-8

First published in Great Britain by Macmillan London Limited.

First U.S. edition

10 9 8 7 6 5 4 3 2 1

THE EXECUTOR

ONE

Keith Calder stepped, rather guiltily, over the threshold of his shop. He expected to find his partner, Wallace James, presiding fussily over the guns and fishing tackle and general sporting paraphernalia; or possibly Janet, Wallace's blonde young wife, holding the fort and lending it a much-needed air of glamour.

Instead, he found his own wife, Molly, demonstrating pigeon-decoys to a spindly youth. In accordance with custom they exchanged no more than a nod. Keith waited patiently until a deal was finalised. He wrapped the awkwardly-shaped purchase while Molly made change.

The bell pinged at last and they had the shop to themselves. Keith kissed his wife, but his first thought was for his daughter. School was out for the summer. 'Who's looking after Deborah?' he asked.

It was not Molly's habit to answer a direct question with equal directness. 'Wal had to go into Edinburgh to fetch some clay pigeons for tomorrow's competition,' she said. 'They didn't come with the bus as promised.'

'That wasn't—'

5

'I'm telling you,' Molly said sternly. 'And Janet wanted to go along with him. She wants to get a coat and some blouses while the sales are on.'

'I asked—'

'So I said I'd look after the shop if they'd take Deb along and get her some new shoes for school.'

'Was Wal looking peeved?' Keith asked.

'He was, rather. Keith, did you have to go off for three days with hardly a word?'

'When somebody pays nearly four thou' for a gun, the least I can do is to deliver it to him and help him settle down with it.'

'So you said. And I told Wal. And he said it didn't take half the working week and that if you brought all the money back with you, he'd eat it. Did you, Keith?'

'Bring back the cash? Most of it, more or less. I got him to trade in a German wheellock from about seventeen forty.'

'In good working order?'

'Well, no. You know how much a good wheellock can fetch.'

'That's what was worrying me.'

'The chain had broken at some time – during an emergency, to judge from the signs—'

'Oh well. You can repair that,' Molly said thankfully.

'—so the owner had had to use it as a club.'

'Keith! Wal will have kittens if it's not repairable.'

'It'll repair.'

'And I bet you weren't doing what you said all the time,' Molly said. 'You were shooting pigeon.'

'I was not.'

'Or rabbits.'

'I gave him a hand getting rid of some mink which had been preying on his pheasant poults,' Keith said.

6

'That was all.'

'Wal—'

'Never mind Wal,' Keith said irritably. 'I started this business with my own capital and I'll take a couple of days off when I feel like it without asking Wal's permission.'

'I thought you were equal partners.'

'We are. But I'm more equal than he is. Have you ever known me show less profit on the antique guns and the repairs than he does on the shop?'

'Well, no. But Wal says you tie up a hell of a lot more capital. I'm only repeating what Wal says. Which reminds me. Mr Enterkin wants to see you, urgently.'

Keith blinked. The connection was obscure. 'What about?' he asked.

'Old Robin Winterton's dead. Didn't you hear? It was on the news. It happened on Monday night. He was alone in the house and somebody broke in and hit him on the head. The police think he disturbed a burglar. His wife came home late and found him lying there, dead.'

'Ah,' Keith said. All was explained. Mr Winterton's collection of antique arms was superb. 'They didn't get away with any of his guns, did they?'

'Not that I've heard. The papers were vague about what was taken.'

'You'd have heard.' The important issue dealt with, Keith was free to think about the death of an old friend. 'Poor devil. Still, he was in his seventies. He'd had his money's-worth out of life.'

'I doubt if you'll still say that when you've had your four-score and ten.'

'Possibly not. But, when we had old Brutus put down, Robin said that he wished he could count on

7

somebody doing as much for him.'

'You won't go buying all those guns?' Molly asked anxiously.

'I couldn't. They'll fetch the earth. But there are one or two pieces. . . .'

'Now, Keith—'

'Not the cream of the collection, but good stuff. I found them for him and I've always regretted not buying them myself. Any coffee going? I'm starved.'

'The percolator's on in the back shop.'

When Keith came back with his coffee, Molly was putting down the phone. 'Mr Enterkin would like to see you at three this afternoon, prompt and without fail. I said you'd be there.'

'But—' Keith wanted to reach his workshop and start work on the wheellock. Or take a gun out in pursuit of the pigeon.

'But first,' Molly said firmly, 'you can take over here. If I don't get some shopping in, there'll be nothing to eat tonight.'

Keith sighed. He knew when he was beaten. 'Well, be quick,' he said, on principle rather than with any real hope.

'And I might get my hair done if Maggie can fit me in. You can have my sandwiches.' As she turned in the door Keith saw her for an instant, backlit by the sun. Her thirty-five years sat very lightly on her. Then she vanished as though she had never been there.

Keith sighed again. He drank his coffee, served a customer and then went back to his usual occupation of displaying the stock the way he liked to show it, with the shooting equipment to the fore. In summer, Wallace usually gave undue prominence to fishing tackle.

* * *

Molly was, by her own standards, remarkably prompt, so that it was only a little after three when Keith crossed Newton Lauder's square through gentle sunshine. A dank summer had relented at last and, Keith thought, the farmers might for once take what they got and be thankful.

He climbed the barren stairs to Mr Enterkin's office. The plain and elderly receptionist passed him through into the solicitor's sanctum, a room the respectable dignity of which was quite spoiled by a perpetual drift of loose papers. The solicitor never seemed to refer to any of them and Keith suspected that he retained them only as stage props.

Behind his desk, Ralph Enterkin, the plump and balding doyen of Newton Lauder's legal brethren, was fidgeting under the eye of a lady of uncertain but no little age.

Robin Winterton, now deceased, had once, with some reluctance, introduced Keith to the lady whom Keith understood to be his second wife. She had let it be seen that she was not impressed. Keith for his part had thought her a formidable old biddy.

He murmured a few words of condolence. Mrs Winterton looked at him coldly, down a nose which she probably thought of as patrician but which, in Keith's view, was definitely hooked. In a dark fur over a grey suit which Keith judged to be off-the-peg but undoubtedly expensive, and with a single, decorous string of pearls showing, she suggested a more wealthy version of the grandmother who had filled his childhood with awe. Keith, who went everywhere in stout, country clothes, ready at any time to take part in a shoot or to help with a little keepering, felt that she expected him to stand behind her chair, but he dropped

9

into the empty chair which had evidently been placed for him and looked enquiringly at the solicitor.

'We gather,' Mr Enterkin said, 'that you have heard about the unfortunate decease of Mr Winterton.'

'Molly told me.'

The widow's response to Keith's words of sympathy had been a sniff. Now she sniffed again, but this time the sniff, instead of a rebuff, was clearly a token tear shed for her late husband. Mrs Winterton seemed to favour her nose as a means of communicating her emotions.

'It would appear,' Mr Enterkin resumed, 'that Mr Winterton was killed on the spur of the moment by an intruder. That being so, confirmation of his will need not be unduly delayed. It would be prudent to await the outcome of the necessary enquiry in the sheriff court. However, as his solicitor I thought that some preliminary discussion would not be wasted.'

'Anything I can do,' Keith said vaguely. 'I suppose, as his executor, you want to discuss the disposal of his guns?'

Mr Enterkin frowned at him. 'You are not making yourself clear,' he said. 'Or, if you are, I must be being obtuse. Would you mind rephrasing that last remark?'

Keith thought that he had made himself perfectly clear, but he knew better than to argue with the old pedant. 'I was supposing,' he said, 'that you, acting as executor of the late Mr Winterton's will, wanted my help in disposing of his collection of guns.'

'That is what I thought you were supposing,' said Mr Enterkin. 'And there's only one thing wrong with it. I'm not his executor. You are.'

'Me?'

'Don't you remember? About nine years ago, when

10

he made a fresh will. In this very office. He asked you whether you were agreeable to being named executor and you said that you were.'

Keith felt himself flush. 'I'd forgotten,' he said humbly. 'At the time, it seemed to be one of those things which'll never happen.'

'Well,' said Mr Enterkin, 'the moment is upon us.'

'I have never understood,' Mrs Winterton said suddenly, shattering the discussion like a stone through glass, 'why my husband chose this . . . gun-person to be his executor.'

'Nor, as a matter of fact, have I,' Mr Enterkin said patiently. 'It was unusual, not to say improper, and I tried to dissuade him. But he was concerned about the disposal of his collection—'

'His old guns and things? You don't have to worry about them any more.'

Keith felt a cold sweat of apprehension break out on him. This was a very odd way to refer to a valuable collection. 'We don't?'

Mrs Winterton shook her head. 'Certainly not. They have all gone, and a good riddance too! I was going to call my son to come and take them away and dump them somewhere. But yesterday afternoon quite a respectable man came to the door. He gave me two hundred pounds for them and took them away in a van.' She nodded, in satisfaction with herself.

Mr Enterkin was the first to break the silence. For once his careful articulation had deserted him. 'Those guns were . . . are worth . . . how much would you say, Keith?'

'There were items in that collection,' Keith said slowly, 'the likes of which have never come on the market before, so I'll not state a figure offhand.

11

Enough to make Mrs Winterton a very wealthy lady, that's all I'll say for now.'

The widow seemed to be stumped for a moment but she made a quick recovery. 'You've said more than enough already,' she snapped, 'and I wish to hear no more of it. I am just not interested. All I wanted was to get rid of the things.' She glared defiantly from one man to the other. 'Those guns ruined my marriage. Whenever I wanted company, my husband would disappear among those insufferable guns.' (Keith found himself nodding. He would have done the same.) 'It was as if he had had a mistress, but worse, because I could soon have settled a mistress's hash if I had chosen to do so. Understand me, if those guns were worth ten times as much as the crown jewels, I still wouldn't care about the money. I'm glad they've gone,' she finished. 'I can manage on the money Robin left.'

Keith looked up at the ceiling and wished that he were somewhere else. Anywhere else.

'I'm afraid you can't,' Mr Enterkin said. 'Because yours was a late marriage and took place after Mr Winterton retired, his pension died with him. His assets consisted almost entirely of the collection. There may be some money in the bank—'

'There should be a thousand or more,' Keith said. 'Unless he made any substantial purchases recently. I sold a good jezail for him last month.'

'I advised Mr Winterton to open a joint account marked "Either or Survivor",' Mr Enterkin said. 'If he did so, then any money in it is yours. Apart from that he had, as far as I am aware, no other money whatever. Not even life assurance.'

'You must be wrong,' said the widow blandly. 'Or else he was mad.'

'Neither,' said Mr Enterkin. 'Explain, Keith.'

The widow switched her cold glare to Keith, who cleared his throat. 'I knew Mr Winterton for nearly twenty years,' he said. 'He came to see me about a pepperbox pistol and asked me some pointed questions about trends in the values of old guns. He had come by some guns through inheritance, and this had stimulated him to buy others. I told him that his family guns were of considerable value, and that his later purchases had gone up. I helped him to do his sums. He was a widower at the time but earning good money. He reckoned that antique guns, carefully bought, would show a better return than almost any other investment.

'So, until his retirement, all his spare cash went into the collection. He looked on it as an easy way to provide for the future without giving up a hobby which was beginning to grip him. In fact, he became very expert – not just on values but on history and technicalities forby. The market dipped once or twice, but in the long run he was well satisfied. Latterly, of course, he was selling an occasional gun to maintain your standard of living.'

The widow seemed to have shrunk inside her unseasonable fur, but she was undefeated. 'I shall sell Halleydane House and its contents,' she said. 'At least Robin owned it outright. I still own a small house in Portobello from my first marriage and the tenants are leaving in December. I shall move back there. It is not such a good address as Halleydane House but. . . .'

Her voice tailed off. Mr Enterkin was shaking his head, pouting his lips in the moue which always reminded Keith of a suckling piglet. 'I'm afraid you still don't understand,' he said sadly. 'I had hoped that your son would be here,' he added.

Mrs Winterton snorted. 'Young man,' she said (Mr Enterkin brightened at hearing himself so described), 'I do not need my son with me, interfering. He has not been to see me since his stepfather died and I can manage without him now. In any case, he is not concerned in this.'

'Your stepson, then.'

'Certainly not him. I may have been kept in the dark so far, but I am perfectly capable of understanding whatever you care to tell me now.'

Although seated, Mr Enterkin managed to draw himself up with dignity. 'Very well,' he said. 'I will make the matter as clear as I can. Your late husband's assets were almost entirely in kind rather than in cash. And he was well aware that you still owned the house in Portobello. Accordingly, he directed that all his assets – comprising Halleydane House and its contents including the collection of antique firearms – be sold. After payment of all debts and duties, he left a specific and generous sum of money to his son by his first marriage, a similar sum to his married daughter in Canada and the remainder to yourself. In effect, of course, this meant that the capital transfer tax payable on those two legacies would have come out of your share of the estate, but you would still have been exceptionally well provided for.

'The position now has changed considerably. Due to your ill-advised and, I may say, quite illegal action, it would seem that there are insufficient assets to meet the bequests to your stepson and stepdaughter. In fact, I stand open to correction but I would suppose that there will be a considerable shortfall. Anything realised from the sale of assets, therefore, would go to them. And, since you had not the least right to sell anything before

14

antiques which he can often buy for far less than the real value and resell to whichever dealer gives the best price for that category of goods.'

'Oh, very well.' Mrs Winterton thought for a few seconds. 'He had no beard or moustache. He was slightly in need of a shave. I don't mean that he had omitted to shave that day,' she explained. 'If that had been the case I should never have let him into the house. But he had the kind of black hair which produces a blue chin within a few hours. He had a round face. And that's all I can remember.'

'Not the colour of his eyes?'

'No.'

'What can you remember about his van?' Keith asked.

'Just a grey van, neither very large nor very small.'

'And his voice?'

'Deep. One of those affected accents you hear such a lot of in these parts. A Scotsman trying to sound English.'

Keith nodded. The working and lower middle class Edinburgh accent can sound affected to the stranger who only mixes with the upper crust.

'Do you know the man?' Mr Enterkin asked anxiously.

'I can think of several who might fit the description,' Keith said. 'Mrs Winterton, tell us everything that happened.'

'The man asked me, very politely, whether I had any antiques which I might be prepared to sell. I said that I had no intention of parting with my treasures but that my husband had left a lot of old guns. I took him to look at them. He said he'd give me a hundred and fifty pounds and take them off my hands. I was only too

17

happy to be rid of the things but I thought that I might as well see how far he would go. I said that I was sure that they were worth more than that. He said that today's market was very uncertain but that he'd taken a fancy to me because I reminded him of his mother, so he'd go to two hundred pounds. The reference to his mother nearly made me change my mind,' Mrs Winterton said loftily, 'but I decided to accept his offer despite his attempt at familiarity.'

Keith switched back to the solicitor. 'That was fraud, wasn't it?' he demanded.

The solicitor pouted again. 'If those were the exact words, probably not. If he stated or implied that those guns were worth only the sum paid, there were no witnesses to the statement. But in any case, Keith, that's not a good line to follow.'

'Why not?'

'Because, if they've already been resold—'

'Which they probably have,' Keith said. 'Especially if this was a put-up job. I can well imagine one of the big dealers sending his pet knocker along to see if he can't grab them both a thief's bargain.'

'—which, as you say, they probably have, the second purchaser could well have a valid title to them and all you could do would be to sue the – er – knocker for the shortfall. On the other hand, Mrs Winterton did not have the right to sell them in the first place. They were not hers to sell. Accordingly, the sale did not take place and thus any subsequent sale was equally invalid and could be upset.'

'That sounds a little more hopeful,' Keith said. 'Not much, but a little. Now all we've got to do is to trace the dealer and every subsequent purchaser and prove to a court how little money changed hands in the first

18

transaction and how much the guns are really worth.'

'You're over-simplifying,' Mr Enterkin said, 'but that will do to be getting on with.'

'I'm so glad,' Keith said. 'Mrs Winterton, was there a name on the van?'

'None that I noticed.'

'There probably wouldn't be,' Keith said. 'How did he pack the guns? Carefully, I hope.'

'Very. He had a stack of old newspapers in the van and he wrapped them all individually.'

'You watched him? Then you must have seen whether he already had some goods in the van.'

For some reason the question seemed to disconcert the widow. She took her time thinking. 'I did watch him,' she said at last. 'After all, I wanted to be sure that he took nothing away but the guns. As far as I can remember, the van was empty except for the newspapers and a box he packed the long guns into.'

'What sort of box?' Keith asked quickly.

She looked at him in surprise. 'Why does it matter?'

'It took the long guns,' Keith explained, 'so it must have been all of five feet long. You don't get ordinary packing-cases that length, so if that's what it was he must have come prepared.'

'It wasn't a packing-case,' she said. 'I remember now. It was very dark oak with brass fittings.'

'Pannelled? Carved?'

'It certainly had panels,' she said. 'I seem to remember some carving. A date, I think, and some initials. And now, I must go. My son is picking me up in a few minutes.'

'Then we still have a few minutes,' Keith said. He used them to probe for more details about the visiting dealer, but without success.

The widow seemed subdued. When she got up to go, she looked up into Keith's face in a manner which held a hint of pathos. 'You will do your best for me, Mr Calder?'

'Of course,' Keith said.

She shook hands with the solicitor. 'I would like to check the inventory,' she said. 'I think the only copy was with the will. Could I borrow it, please?'

'I'll send it to you,' Mr Enterkin said.

Keith held the door for her and refrained from slamming it. 'Old bitch,' he said as he resumed his seat.

'And you were late,' Mr Enterkin said grumpily. 'You left me at her mercy for what seemed like years.'

'Aristocrat talking down to the tradesmen until she needed help,' Keith said. 'Then suddenly she was a poor old widow-woman needing help from the big strong man. I bet she gave poor Robin a hell of a life. I was dying to call her "My poor Mrs Winterton", just for the pleasure of seeing her face. But, as it is, I suppose I'll have to help her.'

'Of course. That's why Mr Winterton appointed you his executor, just in case trouble should arise. He could as easily have appointed me, specifying that the selling of the collection be entrusted to you. That would have been the normal thing to do. But you have a reputation for going into battle when things go wrong. Do you think you'll be able to track down the dealer?' Mr Enterkin asked.

'If he was bona fide, and not some crook who knew about the collection and the death, yes for sure. All the knockers for a hundred miles around have brought me guns at one time or another. Trouble is, it may take time to track down the ones who fit that description and find out which one might have been using a grey van yesterday.'

20

'Time is against us,' Mr Enterkin pointed out. 'In time, some of those guns may have changed hands over and over again.'

'That's what's in my mind,' Keith said. 'So we'll try a few short-cuts. While I go and see Sir Peter Hay, would your receptionist make some phone-calls on my behalf? She could ring every antique-dealer in the yellow pages and tell them that I have a client who wants to exhibit some early muskets appropriately. I want to be told immediately if an antique dower chest comes on the market.'

'What might a dower chest be?'

'Exactly what she described as being in the van.'

'Clever,' Mr Enterkin commented. He made a note.

'The son she was talking about,' Keith said. 'Presumably he wouldn't be the Michael Winterton I've seen competing at field trials.'

'I know nothing of field trials, but Michael is Mr Winterton's son by his first wife. He's a veterinary surgeon over Dunbar way. Mrs Winterton's son by her first husband is a Steven Clune.' There was something in Mr Enterkin's voice which suggested that Steven Clune did not rank among his favourite people.

When Keith walked back across the square, he saw the old lady being helped into the front passenger seat of a recent but modest car by a lanky man, rather younger than himself, with blond hair and, Keith saw when he smiled, very uneven teeth. This, he presumed, was Steven Clune. There seemed to be nothing about him, except perhaps his choice of clothes which were more suited to Chelsea than to the Scottish Borders, to have aroused Mr Enterkin's displeasure.

Keith walked past, ready to exchange a signal of greeting, but Mrs Winterton looked through him.

* * *

The Calders, as a matter of principle, made a special effort to take each evening's meal in a civilised manner. Other meals might be taken individually as snacks, in the kitchen with books or papers on the table, or even in front of the television, but at dinner they remembered their manners. They dined early to suit Deborah's bed-time, but they dined in the dining room of Briesland House, on a polished table carefully set with glass and silver, and cups for their coffee instead of mugs. Life might never offer Deborah a chance to be a lady, but if the chance arrived she would know how to behave.

Polite conversation, avoiding slang or dialect, was therefore required and, lacking any other burning topic of the day, Keith told them about Mrs Winterton's folly. His two ladies were well aware of the values which antique guns can attain and were suitably appalled.

'Then I went up to see Sir Peter,' Keith said. 'I asked him to find out whether any knockers had visited the big houses in that area lately, and whether anybody had sold a dower chest to one of them.'

Molly nodded. It went without saying. Sir Peter Hay was not only their patron and mentor, he was also on visiting terms with all the households likely to attract a knocker's attention. 'Can he help?' she asked.

'He's going to try. I'll go into Edinburgh tomorrow to see what I can sniff out – make it all right with Wallace, will you? – he eats out of your hand – and I'll phone you from time to time to see whether anything's turned up.'

'Can I come with you, Dad?' Deborah asked quickly.

'May I,' Keith corrected. 'Are you sure you want to? You'll be bored.'

'I do want to. Please.'

'If it's all right with your mother,' Keith said.

'Take her along,' Molly said. 'Janet couldn't get her any school shoes. . . .'

'All right. I am not trailing her up and down Princes Street,' Keith said firmly, 'but if we happen to park outside a shoe shop I'll do my best.'

Deborah had paid no attention to the exchange. She knew that she would go with her father. She had dogged Keith's footsteps ever since she could toddle. As a result, she knew more about guns than did many a dealer. 'What's so special about Mr Winterton's collection?' she asked.

Molly got up to serve the sweet. 'And why wouldn't you give Mr Enterkin an estimate of its value?' she asked over her shoulder. 'I know you kept his inventory up to date.'

'Good question,' Keith said. 'And I'll tell you. But you must swear to keep it under your hats. I promised old Robin I'd keep mum. His death changes things. But if word gets around, there'll be more than ourselves chasing after it. If the collection's still missing in a few days' time we may want a blast of publicity, just to make it difficult to dispose of. Until then, not a whisper.

'Now, ask me what's the most valuable gun in the world.'

Deborah quivered with excitement but she went along with the game. 'All right, Dad. What's the most valuable gun in the world?'

'I haven't the faintest idea,' Keith said.

'Och, you!'

'Well, I haven't. The value of something isn't what the last fool paid for it, it's what the next fool's going to pay, and who can predict a thing like that? The really

23

valuable guns are valuable because they're so rare that nothing like them comes on the market more than once in a blue moon.

'But if I was asked to guess at the most valuable gun in the world—'

'We're asking you,' Deborah said.

'Well, I'd be hard put to it to answer. But I'd probably say that it would be one of the original Scottish long guns. The musket with the snaphaunce lock and ball trigger.'

'Did Mr Winterton have one of those?' Molly asked.

'He had two.'

'But, Dad,' Deborah said, 'in that article you wrote for *Scottish Field*, you said that there were less than thirty in the world and that half of those, the ones abroad, had never been authenticated.' She screwed up her face with the effort of memory. That was Molly's trick and once again Keith was reminded of the resemblance between mother and daughter. 'You said that there were only seventeen in this country, two in the Tower of London, two in the Wallace Collection and the rest, owned by the Countess of Seafield, were lent to the Museum of Antiquities. All the others were destroyed by the English after the 'forty-five rebellion was put down. You said,' she added.

'That's where you're wrong, Clever-clogs,' her father said sternly. 'You remember too much or too little. You missed out a half-dozen very important little words. Know what they are?'

Deborah shook her head.

'I said, "As far as is generally known", which is all you can ever say about such things. I'll tell you what happened. After Montrose was betrayed by the O'Neills, some of the Scots families who'd been fighting

24

for Montrose under Colkitto, particularly the McDonalds, Campbells and Crawefords, fled with their families to Ireland by way of Dumbarton. Most of them settled down around Limavaddy in County Tyrone, which is still known locally as "Scotch Corner".'

'Is that where Mr Winterton came from?' Deborah asked.

'His first wife did, and she had a legacy from her family of some money and the contents of a house, including some old guns. Most of them were humdrum, but they included two Scottish snaphaunce muskets, both by James Low of Dundee. He was perhaps the premier maker of the time after the Laird of Grant's own gunsmith, Duthill. One of them, probably the more valuable, is all-brass and dated sixteen thirteen, which makes it earlier even than the one by Robert Allison in the Tower of London, which belongs to the Queen. The other has a wooden stock inlaid with silver and a steel barrel and lockwork inlaid with gold and it's absolutely beautiful.'

'Couldn't you even guess what they'd be worth, then?' Molly asked.

'How could I? No such gun has ever been on the open market. I can think of at least one top American collector who'd cheerfully hand the vendor a blank cheque and tell him to fill in the amount for himself. And the museums would still be trying to outbid him.'

'And you're trying to get them back for that nasty old woman,' Molly said.

'That does stick in my gullet a bit, but an executor has his duties. Anyway, in my book they're national treasures, but if they've got to be sold I want the kudos of selling them.'

'And your commission.'

25

'That too. It's provided for in the will. But it's Winterton's own son I'm sorry for. As it is, his legacy's less than it should be because Winterton's will was out-of-date as values go and, after all, the guns did come from his mother's estate. If I don't recover them, he won't even get a half of what his father intended.

'And now,' Keith said, 'if we've finished, there's still enough light left for me to go out. There's a pigeon been waking me up in the mornings, eternally broadcasting the letter R in Morse code, and I want him in the freezer before he drives me mad.'

'I'm coming with you,' Deborah said firmly.

'All right, Toots. Get your four-ten; we'll lie in wait for him at the bottom of the garden.'

Molly, who had hoped for some help with the washing-up, gritted her teeth but held her peace.

TWO

A Mini was pulling out from a meter under the looming mass of Edinburgh Castle and Keith slid the hatchback neatly into its place.

'Come on, Toots,' he said. 'Unhook yourself. We're going walkabout.'

He fed the meter all that it would accept and they set off hand in hand up Johnston Terrace. At the beginning of Lawnmarket, Keith stopped. 'I'm going into Angus Pride's shop,' he said. 'It'll just be talk. You take a walk along High Street and then double back round the Grassmarket. You know the way?'

'Of course I do,' his daughter said impatiently. Being the prime tourist area, it was rich in antique shops.

'Look into all the antique shops and see if you can spot a dower chest. That's a long box of very dark oak, probably with a big, brass lock and fittings. The top and front would be in three panels each. It would have a date and two sets of initials.'

'And if they have any guns?'

'Come back and tell me.' He handed Deborah his wallet. He believed in letting her learn from her

27

mistakes. If she blew this one, it would still be a lesson cheap at the price. 'But if you see one which you think's underpriced, buy it. You understand?'

Deborah nodded, wide-eyed.

'If you pass a shoe shop, get yourself some school shoes. You've a spare pair of socks in your pocket. Shoes must go on over both pairs of socks, got it?'

'Yes, Dad.'

'Off you go, then. Meet me at Mr Pride's shop as soon as you're done. You remember where it is?'

'Where we bought the Von Dreyse rifle.'

'Right.'

He watched her out of sight, a slim figure beginning to move with the confidence of womanhood, of knowing that she is to be admired. He would have to speak to her about that provocative swing of the hips. She was at the shooting-up stage and her height was always surprising him. He shrugged and went into Angus Pride's shop.

Molly, meanwhile, was on the phone to Wallace. 'Keith's gone into Edinburgh,' she said. 'He's Robin Winterton's executor and something's gone wrong. Somebody conned the widow into selling the gun collection for peanuts and Keith's trying to get them back.'

'I t-take it that he's earning a fee?' Wallace was the money-man of the partnership.

'I suppose so,' Molly said. 'Do executors get a fee? I know he gets a commission on selling the guns.'

'Well, whatever, let him get on with it. This is the quiet season and we d-don't want him getting bored. Last occasion that he found time lying heavy on his hands, he started building a blasted wheellock for

28

competition shooting and we hardly got any work out of him for months.'

'We got some useful publicity out of it,' Molly pointed out.

'Not enough. K-keep him out of mischief until the rush of guns for overhaul starts. And try to stop him buying any of the guns for the business without showing me the inventory first. Otherwise he'll get up to his usual trick.'

'What usual trick?' Molly asked curiously. After all these years, she was still learning.

'Juggling the values. Buying for his personal collection at a low price and making it back for the client by pushing up the ones he buys for the firm to where our profit's minimal. Don't let him think I don't know, that's all. I don't mind him cheating the tax man – not a lot – but I'm damned if he's doing it at my expense.'

Molly hung up. She bit her lip. That was very naughty of Keith. But it was clever.

The antique shop was quiet. Angus Pride handed over to his assistant, a girl so young that Keith suspected that she was either a YOP or a WEEP and therefore heavily subsidised by the Manpower Services Commission.

From the street, the shop looked small; but it rambled away behind the adjoining shops and into the upper floors of the building so that the casual visitor, intending no more than to glance around, was easily trapped into spending an hour or more in exploration.

Angus took Keith upstairs to where, at the back of yet another showroom or gallery, he had his own office.

'Those damned stairs'll be the death of me,' he grumbled, settling his stomach more comfortably on his knees. 'Now, Keith, what are you after?' Pale blue eyes stared suspiciously from under his white eyebrows.

'An old lady I know was conned by a knocker the day before yesterday,' Keith said. He repeated Mrs Winterton's description. 'I've jotted down any names I could think of which might fit, allowing for an error or two on her part.'

Angus Pride ran his eyes down the list. 'You're not far off,' he said. 'I could maybe add a name but it wouldn't help you – the man I'm thinking of was in Fife the last few days. You can forget most of the rest. This one's in hospital. The next spent all week trailing round the dealers, trying to unload a set of chairs he paid too much for. The next was in Inverness, following up a story about a set of claymores. The next – George Baker – wears a beard these days. Vague as your old dame seems to be she could hardly have missed that.'

'When did you see him last?' Keith asked. Beards can be removed.

'This morning. And Snotty Harris uses a black Rolls-Royce van he converted out of a hearse. That leaves you with Duncan Laurie. Aye, it could be him. He was knocking somewhere south of here, last I heard. Of course, an Edinburgh accent's not much to go on; it could still be somebody working out of Glasgow or Newcastle.'

'I've got to start somewhere,' Keith said. 'Does Duncan Laurie have a grey van?'

'Damned if I know. Parking's difficult around here, so they carry in what they're selling, most times, unless it's huge.'

'Where's his store?'

'Waterman's Lane, off the Cowgate. It still says Frazer's Frozen Foods over the door.'

Keith smiled. 'Thanks, Angus. I owe you a favour.'

'You could sell yon pair of duelling pistols for me,' old Angus said hopefully. He gestured towards a pair of saw-handled pistols with octagonal barrels in a mahogany case.

Keith tried not to smile. 'Are those the ones you bought for the American tourist who turned out to be one of the gang? They're fakes, and not very good ones. I'll not sell them as real. But, if you like, I'll sell them as interesting copies with a story attached to them.'

'The story being how I was had for a sucker?'

'It's that or most of your money down the drain,' Keith said.

'So be it,' Angus said with a sigh. He pursed his soft, pink lips. 'You'll tip me off if anything good comes on the market from Halleydane House?'

Keith looked at him hard and met a return stare from the pale blue eyes. 'What put Halleydane House into your mind?' he asked.

'Come off it, lad,' Angus said. 'You were as thick as thieves with old man Winterton and steered all his money into antique guns. Then, three days after he gets himself topped during a break-in, you're running around in a tizzy and looking for a knocker who underpaid a widow for some guns.'

'I didn't say guns,' Keith protested.

'But you're you,' Angus pointed out. 'You wouldn't be getting in a sweat over snuff-boxes or old china. Rumour has it that there was something very special in the Winterton collection.'

Keith felt himself jump. 'Where did you hear that?' he asked.

'It's true, then? It was just a word that went the rounds. You know how it would be. The owner isn't

31

going to keep his treasure buried for ever. He tells or shows a friend. The friend drops a hint and the word's on the move. You think the knocker was there for a purpose?'

'I've been wondering,' Keith said. 'What do you think?'

'Depends. It depends,' Angus said shrewdly, 'on how well it was known that the old shrew didn't know the value of the guns and would be only too glad to be rid of them. I knew it, but not everyone would. Look at it this way. Somebody gets word that old Winterton has something of great value in his collection. It was well protected?'

'Very,' Keith said. 'A vaulted cellar under the house, steel door and infra-red alarms connected through to the police station.'

'There you are. I've seen the old girl around the auctions – never buying anything, just watching and running the bidding up when she felt safe. Whenever a gun turned up in a sale she'd start grumbling about Winterton's guns. I've heard her, myself, saying that she was going to chuck the lot into the sea. An arrogant old biddy and stupid with it.

'So they wait until her husband's alone in the house and send in a screwsman who knocks him on the head. The police are going to seal off that part of the house, but they'll only look once round the rest of it. The widow has to go on living there, doesn't she?

'Then, first time the place is clear of fuzz for a minute, the tame knocker arrives, rustling a bundle of notes. Likely there were men standing by, and if she hadn't taken the money there'd have been a knife at her throat until she unset the alarms and opened the door.'

'I was wondering along the same lines,' Keith said. 'If you're right, I've got problems. Would Duncan Laurie go along with murder?'

'Likely he would. Anybody'll do anything if the money's right and Duncan's no better than most and worse than a lot of 'em, and he's got money-troubles just now. He went to court over payment for a pair of vases which didn't stand up to examination, and he lost. Nothing's worse for a knocker than being short of working capital. Or he might even have not known that there was any connection with the murder, just been sent in to buy.'

Keith stood up. 'I'd better get going,' he said.

'Most of them'll likely be offered to you anyway.'

'Christ! I don't want to buy them,' Keith said. 'I'm Mr Winterton's executor. I just want to get them back for the estate.'

'His executor, are you? Don't forget me, then. I hear there's some good stuff in Halleydane House.'

Keith threaded a careful way through the expensive clutter of the shop. The young girl assistant, abandoning for the moment her true mission of deterring shoplifters, caught him at the door. 'Are you Mr Calder? There's a phone-call . . . .'

'If it's his wife, he isn't here,' Keith said flippantly. Young girls, especially young girls with budding bosoms and round behinds, always brought out the worst in him. 'If it's his girl-friend, I'll take it.'

'I don't know who it is,' the girl said, unsmiling.

Keith took the phone. Molly's voice came through sweet and clear. 'Keith? There are some messages. Mr Enterkin's receptionist rang. She's tried every dealer in the Lothian and Borders yellow pages. Nobody's got a

33

dower chest but they all said they'll call her back if one turns up. But they may not bother. Several of them said that hers wasn't the only enquiry.'

'Fine,' Keith said. 'What else?'

'Sir Peter's phoned his friends for about twenty miles around Halleydane House. A man with a grey van was on the knock a few days ago but nobody sold him a dower chest and nobody seems to have seen him on the day after Mr Winterton was killed. A Mrs Fairlie sold him an ormolu clock. She says there was no dower chest in the van, but the van was definitely grey. And she kept his card.'

'Let me guess,' Keith said. 'Laurie. Right?'

'You are the most maddening person,' Molly said. 'You get all sorts of people sweating blood for you and running up colossal phone bills, and when they come up with the answer you wanted you've already got it. This isn't the first time.'

'I'll try to be stupider in future,' Keith said humbly.

'Don't be silly. And Michael Winterton—'

'The old man's son.'

'—phoned. He wants to get in touch with you. He's in Edinburgh. I said that he might be able to catch you at Angus Pride's shop.'

'He'll have to be quick.'

'Is Debbie all right? Can I speak to her?'

'Right as rain. But she isn't exactly here at the moment. She's getting shoes,' Keith added quickly. That might pacify Molly.

It didn't. 'Keith, you haven't let her go wandering off on her own again? I told you to keep her with you.'

Keith glared at an inoffensive Toby-jug which glared back at him. 'Och, a little responsibility teaches her self-reliance,' he said. 'She'll be back in a minute.'

34

'She's too damn self-reliant already,' Molly said. 'That child is old beyond her years. You go and find her at once and have her call me or I'll never speak to you again.'

'You promise?' Keith said. He hung up quickly.

Outside, still carrying the case of pistols, he looked around. There was no sign of Deborah among the mixed sightseers and shoppers. He knew that Molly was over-cautious and yet, infected with her anxiety, he could not suppress a sense of panic. When a large estate-car drew up beside him and somebody spoke his name, the distraction was a relief. He recognised the face above the steering-wheel by the drooping moustache and the air of ruddy good health as belonging to Michael Winterton, old Robin's son.

'It is Mr Calder, isn't it? Your wife said you might be here. Hop in. I'd like a word.' He had a voice which could only have emanated from at least one expensive school.

'You hop out,' Keith said.

'I'm on yellow lines. We could drive round the block.'

'No, we couldn't. One, I'm waiting for my young daughter. Two, I'm your father's executor and I don't think I should be seen to be having private conversations with one of the beneficiaries. Three, there's little or no traffic. Four, as soon as my daughter turns up, I'm off in a hurry. And, five, if a traffic-warden approaches, we can see him ... her ... oh, damn! ... it, a hundred yards off.'

Michael Winterton grunted and got out of the car. He was a man of about Keith's age or slightly less but several inches taller. His heavy frame showed no trace of excess fat but, close to, the signs of dissipation were

35

present. A nerve was twitching beside his mouth and when they shook hands his skin was hot and moist. Keith decided that a murdered father was enough to make any man nervous.

The back seat of the estate-car was folded down and Keith saw that two good-looking labradors were sprawled at ease in the generous space provided. 'Nice dogs,' Keith said. 'The sporting press tells me that you've been having your wins with them.'

Winterton smiled fleetingly. 'The yellow's a granddaughter of Septimus Spry. You used to own Septimus, didn't you?'

'That's right.' It was Keith's turn to smile. Sep had made him a lot of money in stud fees in his day.

Few things establish a quicker empathy than a common interest in dogs. Winterton seemed to relax. He leaned an elbow on the roof of the car and Keith did the same, resting the weight of the cased pistols. The roof was still wet from a car-wash.

'I don't want to compromise you,' Winterton said. 'Just a quick word. Is it true that that charming and intelligent old lady, my revered stepmother, has let the most important part of my father's property go for a song?'

'That seems to be the case,' Keith said carefully.

'In that eventuality, what's left comes to me?'

'And your sister,' Keith reminded him. 'You'd better speak to Ralph Enterkin, but that's how I understand it. Subject to certain questions about capital transfer tax.'

Winterton looked away. 'How long is all this going to take? Don't misunderstand me. I'm not short of a bob or two. But I'm in business for myself and I'm planning an expansion. It makes a big difference if I can safely

36

take the more expensive short-term loan as against a cheaper loan that would have to run full-term.'

It occurred belatedly to Keith that he should have expressed his condolences, but the moment seemed to have passed. He was also remembering that, on the few previous occasions when he had been within speaking-distance of Michael Winterton, the vet had preferred to converse with those whom he considered to be his social equals. Keith himself rarely thought in terms of class and, whenever he encountered it, his hackles rose.

'I've started preparing an inventory of the estate,' he said, 'but I can hardly start distributing it before the police have finished their investigations.'

'Why not, for God's sake? Surely the matters are separate.'

Keith realised that he might already have gone too far. He tried to back-pedal. 'The lawyers could argue that I might be handing out legacies to somebody who was disqualified.'

'Are you suggesting,' Winterton enquired angrily, 'that my stepmother or I – or my sister – might have burgled the house and killed my father?'

'Certainly not. But the lawyers might argue that the possibility existed. Presumably if there isn't a trial there'll be an enquiry. That should settle the matter. Then again, your father's will specified that all his assets be sold. You don't sell a place like Halleydane House in two minutes.'

Winterton sighed and decided not to embroil himself in argument with the hypothetical lawyers. 'If I could just be sure that I had the proceeds of the sale coming. . .'

'I wouldn't go borrowing on the strength of it,' Keith said. 'Capital transfer tax will be taken off before any

37

legacies are handed out. If the Inland Revenue decides that tax is payable on the real value of the estate, everything realised will be gobbled up.'

Keith had forgotten about Deborah. Now he realised that she was pulling at his coat. 'I got shoes,' she said. 'And Granny Howett had saved you the lock from a Tower Musket. I gave her four pounds for it. Was that all right?'

She gave Keith his wallet and then handed him the lock, wrapped in her handkerchief. Keith put on one of the cotton gloves from his pocket before accepting it. The Calders knew that, while a delicate piece of the gunsmith's art might have the acid fingerprints of centuries etched into it, there was no sense in adding to them. 'Very reasonable,' he said.

'She wanted ten but I beat her down.'

Michael Winterton looked at the device without interest. 'You knew, if anyone did, that my father had some valuable Scottish guns,' he said. 'Could they have reached the antique shops already? I ask because there's one in a window near here, in West Bow.'

'It's only a fowling-piece,' Deborah said haughtily. 'About eighteen seventy. It's been there for weeks. And I'm not surprised,' she added, 'because they're asking far too much.'

'Sorry I spoke,' Winterton said faintly.

Deborah waved a hand. 'That's all right. You weren't to know.'

'We'll have to be going,' Keith said. He pointed over Winterton's shoulder. 'And there's a warden beyond that van, arguing with the driver.'

'I'm off,' Winterton said. He got into his car. The dogs snuffled at his neck and he pushed them away.

'See what you can do to hurry things along, will you,

38

Mr Calder?' He slammed his door and drove off.

'You are silly, Dad,' Deborah said. 'There's no traffic-warden.'

'I know, but at least it got rid of him. We have an urgent visit to make. On the way we'll make a little detour, drop the boxes in the car and feed the meter.'

The Cowgate dips to pass under George IV Bridge. As they walked through its echoes and between the backs of tall buildings in reddish stone, Keith asked, 'If that fowling-piece had been half the price, would you have bought it?'

'Of course,' Deborah said firmly. 'Why not?'

'Most girls, let loose with their dad's wallet, would make a bee-line for the nearest boutique.'

'Most girls are wet,' Deborah said. 'Boys are better, as long as they don't get soppy.'

'Sometimes I worry about you,' Keith said. 'I don't know whether I've got a son or a daughter. You have the worst vices of both. Anyway, you'd have been done. Have a look at that fowling-piece next time we go that way. It's a fake.'

'Really, Dad? I'll swear the barrel and action are genuine. I saw that it had been re-stocked, but I was sure that it had been done during the period. I was wrong, was I?'

'It was re-stocked about the time you were born. But don't feel too badly about it, Toots. The ageing was brilliantly done,' Keith said. 'I know, because I did it myself. I was a bit short of funds at the time. Ah, Waterman's Lane.' They turned the corner into a narrow street serving a mixture of tired buildings, mostly of an industrial nature. 'And that looks like the place I want, along on the left with the green sign.' The

39

sight of a phone-box reminded him. 'You phone your mother. Dial one hundred and reverse the charges. When you've finished, follow me up. If you hear any loud noises or see anything you don't like, go back and phone the police?'

'Nine-nine-nine?'

'You've got it.'

The signboard for Frazer's Frozen Foods was on the gable of a small public house. Keith guessed that the sign applied to the adjacent building, which was set back just enough to allow for a small yard where a grey van was parked. Looking through the back windows, he saw that the van seemed to be empty except for a stack of crumpled newspapers. The uppermost was the front page of a *Sun* still bearing the newsagent's scribble for the delivery boy. It looked like Donelly.

After the bustle of Edinburgh's crowded streets the lane was unnaturally quiet. Keith moved over quickly to double doors painted a flaking green. There was no bell so he banged with his fist. There was no answer or sound of movement. He wondered where to go from there. As an afterthought, he tried the handle and found that the door was unlocked.

The lane was still as quiet as a graveyard. Keith gave the heavy door a push and slipped inside. His first impression was that the store was tidy but that neatly ranged around the painted brick walls were the unsold items which Duncan Laurie had picked up – valueless inclusions with job lots, broken furniture awaiting repair or cannibalisation and odd numbers of chairs kept in the hope of completing the set. Opposite, a workbench bore tools, polishes and a tallcase clock in process of undergoing repair to a damaged corner. The place smelt of new polish and mouldering upholstery.

He moved forward. The door and a wormy wardrobe had been hiding the horror in the corner. Keith's first impulse was to run but he steeled himself and stepped forward, placing his feet with care.

Duncan Laurie had sold Keith a powder-flask and a walking-stick gun and had, from time to time, offered him other less tempting, faked or possibly stolen pieces. So Keith knew his face and could recognise its profile among the mess. And, as if that were not enough, he could smell the knocker's hair-oil even above the odours which accompany a violent death.

Deborah must not see this, or smell it. She would be with him at any moment. But no. Two females on the phone . . . He had a minute or two. More likely an hour or so. He stared.

Laurie had slumped forward over the table which, apparently, he used for his paperwork. The wound was nearly closed, but the head was turned a little to one side, causing the wound to gape below the right ear, and Keith could see that his throat was cut. Blood had sprayed over the tidy shoe-boxes of papers on the table, splattered the nearby wall and dripped to the floor.

Keith heard a sound outside. He darted to the door. Deborah was approaching uncertainly. She sighed with relief when she saw her father.

'Back to the phone,' Keith said. 'Dial nine-nine-nine, ask for the police and tell them to come to Waterman's Lane, the old Frazer's Frozen Foods building. A crime's been committed and that's all you know. Understand?'

Deborah nodded dumbly.

'Go, then.'

He watched her round the corner and then forced himself to go back inside. On the blood-soaked table was a box of old-fashioned razors of the type which would hold a different razor for every day of the week plus a spare. Seven ivory-handled razors seemed to be in place and one lay under the corpse's fingers. It looked like a valuable set although it was hard to tell under so much blood.

One of the shoe-boxes had held receipts but the topmost was indecipherable. Keith would have liked to search further down the box but the risk was too great.

A pocket diary lay near to the dead hand. The back cover had stuck to the table with congealing blood. Keith used a ballpoint pen from his pocket to turn the pages. The entries were not methodical, covering only such appointments and phone-numbers as Duncan Laurie had wanted to remember. The last entry was for two days earlier, the day on which Mrs Winterton had sold her late husband's collection. It said only 'D. Bruce', and underneath, perhaps not even part of the same notation, 'Rutherglen'. Lower still was a vague scrawl which might have been 'Guns'.

Keith uttered the rudest word he could think of. It was a very rude word indeed. He let the diary fall shut. There was a trace of blood on the end of his pen. He wiped it on the palm of his hand and returned it to his pocket.

Against the wall, to one side of the corpse and slightly behind its shoulder, stood an object which, because it had been in his mind, had been familiar and therefore unnoticed. Now he realised that he was looking at a dower chest. It was almost exactly as he had described it to Deborah. In the middle panel of the front was carved a date, 1573, and to either side initials, K.B. on the left and J.L. to the right. As far as Keith could see, it had escaped being spotted with blood; but

42

the blood was already almost black and spots would hardly show on the very dark oak.

He pulled on his cotton gloves and stooped to lift one end of the chest. It was very heavy but he managed to look underneath. On the concrete was a single spot of what looked like blood. He lowered the chest and lifted its lid. It was empty. He sniffed, but if there was a smell of gun-oil he could not detect it.

Keith removed and pocketed his gloves and spent a few more seconds looking around. It seemed important that he try to fix every detail in his memory although his stomach was urging him to leave the place and find somewhere where he could be quietly and privately sick.

When the first police-car arrived he was waiting beside the grey van. Even the van seemed to be blood-spattered, but he realised after a moment that the splashes of burgundy had been made by berries.

The two constables who were the first to arrive were visibly shaken and yet inclined to accept the suicide as a matter of fact and therefore of no great criminal import. The detective sergeant who followed them took a similar view but kept the two Calders waiting anyway while he examined the scene. This was much as Keith had expected. The police, in his experience, considered the convenience of witnesses to be rather less important than their own tea-breaks.

When he judged that the time was ripe, Keith made his move. Deborah, ready to burst with unsatisfied curiosity, was sitting in the back of the panda car playing 'I spy' with one of the constables. Keith stooped to the window. 'I'm going to phone home,' he said, 'and then see whether the pub can't provide a sandwich. It's past this child's lunch-time. And I could use a brandy after what I've just seen.'

'Sergeant said to wait here,' the constable said uneasily. He was not unsympathetic. He could have used a drink himself after seeing all that blood on an empty stomach.

Keith laughed. 'Christ!' he said. 'I'll never be more than twenty yards away and you know who I am. You think I'm going to bolt for it, leaving my business in the lurch and my daughter in your hands, just because I found . . . what I found?'

He turned away without waiting for an answer and walked the few yards to the phone-box. He kept his body between the police-car and the dial in case the constable wondered why he had to call Directory Enquiries before phoning home.

After less than a minute, his call completed, he passed the car again and entered the pub. There are lunch-time pubs and evening pubs and this was one of the latter. The old-fashioned bar was empty except for a bored barmaid whose bleached hair was only one of her defences against the advancing years. She brightened when Keith walked in. She produced sandwiches already wrapped in plastic film and mixed Keith a port-and-brandy – a remedy which he always found settling to a disturbed stomach. Her accent reminded him of Mrs Winterton's description of Duncan Laurie's.

Keith excused himself. In the Gents, before washing, he sniffed his hands. There was something there which stirred a faint memory but he couldn't pin it down. He carefully washed his hands and his pen before returning to the bar.

The barmaid was in a sociable mood. 'Did I hear an

44

ambulance outside?' she .asked. 'Nobody taken ill, I hope.'

Keith thought for a moment before deciding that she would hear the news soon enough. 'It was a police-car. Your neighbour seems to have topped himself.'

'Not Mr Laurie?' She sounded horrified and yet pleased to find drama on her doorstep on a boring day.

'You knew him then? He came in here?'

'Almost every evening. Him and his friend.' She jerked her head. 'Always sat at the corner table and had a pie and a pint. How did he . . . do it?'

'You wouldn't want to know,' Keith said. 'Not a delicately nurtured lady like yourself. Anyway, it'll be in the papers.' He offered her a drink and she poured herself a vodka-and-lemonade, much flattered by the tribute to her upbringing. 'Who was the friend?' he asked.

She shrugged. With her elbows on the bar, her shoulders did not go up; instead, the rest of her went down. 'Called him Mike. An older man. I think he's a french polisher, though why they call him that I don't know, when French he certainly isn't. He works somewhere else during the day but helped Mr Laurie doing up his bits and pieces of furniture in the evenings.'

'You never heard his surname?'

'I may've done. Something Irish.'

Keith remembered the newspapers in the van. Duncan Laurie, dealing largely in delicate *objets d'art*, would have got through a lot of newspapers. He might well have collected those of his friend. 'Donelly?' he suggested.

She snapped her fingers. 'Right,' she said.

'But you don't know where I could find him?'

'Not the faintest, dear.'

Keith took out one of his business cards. 'If he ever comes in here again, give him this. There's a tenner to split between you if he phones me.'

'I'll remember,' she said. 'Come back some time and I'll buy you a drink in return. Not port-and-brandy, though. That's two drinks.'

He bought some lemonade to go with the sandwiches and hurried outside.

A man with a bag, presumably the police surgeon, was just coming out of the store.

THREE

They had finished their picnic in the panda car, sharing the sandwiches with the constable, before the sergeant was ready to interview Keith. The two men moved into the sergeant's car.

The detective sergeant's questions were purely formal. Keith had given some thought to how much he would say and he had decided that he needed police help in tracing the missing guns. He told the sergeant of Mrs Winterton's folly. 'I'd done business with Duncan Laurie in the past,' he explained, 'and I tracked him down from Mrs Winterton's description. So if you come across any antique guns, or indications that they passed through his hands within the last few days, such as a large sums of money. . . .'

'I'll let you know. Suicide doesn't suggest that he'd just pulled off a profitable deal. You didn't interfere with anything?'

'Only to look and see what had happened, and make sure that my guns weren't on open show. Now, can I go? My car's on a meter in Johnston Terrace.'

The sergeant drew a line under his notes. 'If you get a

ticket, contact me,' he said. 'I can give you a note to say that you were delayed by the need to help the police. And a fat lot of good it may or may not do you. You'll get a statement to sign at home. And there'll be an enquiry in the sheriff court. You'll have to give evidence.'

'No trouble,' Keith said. He collected Deborah and hurried away. Once they were out of sight he found another phone-box. This time he really did phone Molly.

During the hour-long drive back to Newton Lauder, Deborah bombarded him with questions. He spelled out the facts as gently as he could. He refused to describe the body. Time enough for the girl to learn about the macabre side of death later. Besides, now that he had had time to believe the horror of the morning, his own stomach was uneasy again. He tried to clear his mind by observing the harvest as they passed by. It was poor but they might save most of it now that fine weather had arrived at last.

He drove straight to Briesland House – Molly's orders had been specific and he was glad to comply. Ever since a lucky venture had enabled him to buy the solid, secluded old house, it had been more to him than a home and a status symbol – it had become a safe refuge in times of trouble, a castle where he was king.

Molly met them in the hall. 'Go and wash,' she told Deborah and her tone was such that Deborah went without argument. Molly turned on Keith. 'Did you let that child see any dead bodies?'

'No, I did not,' Keith said. 'And there was only one.'

Molly moved to the second most important question. 'Have the two of you had anything to eat?'

'Just a couple of sandwiches. And the bobby in the

patrol-car took the lion's share of those.'

'There'll be something hot in ten minutes.' She looked closely at Keith. 'You've had a shock too. Drink this.' She disappeared into the kitchen, leaving Keith standing open-mouthed in the hall with a glass of whisky in his hand. Molly still never failed to surprise him.

He followed her as far as the kitchen door. 'I've got things to do,' he said.

Molly looked up from the frying-pan. 'Do them here. I took you at your word. Mr Enterkin's coming here. Sir Peter will look in if he can. Wallace can't get away, but Janet's coming instead. Now, tell me the worst, quickly, before Deborah comes back.'

In an irreducible minimum of words, and trying hard not to hear his own voice, Keith described the scene.

Molly accepted the facts calmly. She left the frying-pan while she set the kitchen table and put bread in the toaster. 'You don't believe that he killed himself,' she said. 'Do you?'

'No,' Keith said. 'I don't. But how did you know?'

'I could tell from your voice. And you were careful to say that he "seemed to" have killed himself. I'm glad you came home straight away, but why did you? Knowing you, I'd have expected you to hang around in the hope of picking up the trail of the guns.'

Keith blew out a long breath. 'You're getting too damned perceptive! I got away as quickly as I could because I'd already got one clue to where the guns went. And because a forensic scientist will surely see the body and he won't buy suicide any more than I did. While they have a suicide and no mystery, the cops may be satisfied to have a detective sergeant do the necessary and let witnesses go home, but when they're

49

investigating a murder it's a different ball-game. Ranking officers, mobile headquarters, dozens of men. And the man who found the body can just bloody well wait until somebody gets around to deciding that they've got all he knows. I've found a body before now, remember? And I wasn't bloody well hanging around for that. I've got too much to do in a hurry. I'm here and they can talk to me here at my convenience and when I'm good and ready.'

Deborah's feet were heard on the stairs and the subject was dropped in a hurry.

Molly served kidneys, bacon and mushrooms on toast and while they ate she discouraged questions on Deborah's part as being 'ghoulish curiosity'. But when Deborah, after being sworn to secrecy, was despatched to spend what was left of the afternoon with her friend at the nearby market-garden, Molly's own curiosity was let loose.

'Keith, why don't you believe that it was suicide?' she asked.

Keith finished his coffee. 'A lot of little pointers. It didn't look right. His papers were very tidy, yet his blood had spurted all over them. That'd be against nature. There was no note. And a suicide using a sharp blade nearly always makes tentative cuts before he gets up the nerve to do the job.'

'And there weren't any?'

'There were. But one of them, the only one above the line of the main cut, was in an area of unbloodied skin. It was deep but it hadn't bled, so it was made after death. My guess is that the murderer made the tentative cuts as an afterthought. He may even have gone back to do it.'

'What do you think happened?' Molly asked.

50

'My guess is that there was a neat and nasty plot. The murderer walked in and offered to sell Laurie a set of old-fashioned razors. Laurie examined them at his table and while he had one in his hand the murderer, standing behind him, produced another razor and made one quick slash.'

'But he'd get bloodied,' Molly said.

'He could have worn a boiler-suit,' Keith said, 'and rubber gloves – you know how inconspicuous the transparent ones can be – and carried them away in a carrier-bag. He could even have put a clear polythene bag over his head before he struck, just in case.'

The front doorbell chimed suddenly.

'Thank God!' Keith said. 'A few more minutes of your ghoulish curiosity and I'd probably have thrown up. I'll go.'

A battered Land-Rover was parked on the gravel and Sir Peter Hay was standing with his back to the door, admiring the sweep of open country which sloped gently down the valley to the town. His lanky frame was clad in a threadbare kilt and his hair was an untidy mop as usual.

'Come in, Peter.'

Sir Peter looked over his shoulder. 'I overtook your legal pal.'

'Near the town?'

'No. Not far from here.'

'Then we may as well wait,' Keith said. Ralph Enterkin was a notoriously slow driver, often over-taken by farm machinery or old ladies on bicycles.

Mr Enterkin's Rover crawled nervously in at the gate and up the short gravel drive and came to a halt behind the Land-Rover. While the solicitor was hoisting himself carefully out of the driver's seat, Janet James,

Wallace's wife, slipped out of the passenger's door. Her naturally blonde hair was the brightest thing under that day's sun. She seemed quite unaware that her every movement seemed to demand the attention of a camera. Wallace could never understand how he had attracted anything so visually and sexually dazzling and Keith, who had known Janet since her childhood, agreed.

'Wal wanted to keep the car,' she said. 'Then he can follow along if we're still here when the shop shuts.'

'So, of course, I offered my services,' Mr Enterkin said. 'Good afternoon, Sir Peter.'

Keith led them through to his study, a gracious room which never failed to remind him how he had come up in the world, even if he alone knew that the furniture was all reproduction. Molly, after dumping the dishes into soapy water with a promise of later action, joined the party and Keith had to fetch another chair before settling himself in the swivel chair behind the desk.

'Before I bring you up to date,' he said, 'let's run over the events of the week and fill in the gaps.

'On Monday, I left on a business trip. That evening, Mrs Winterton went out. Where?'

'To the theatre,' Mr Enterkin said, 'with two old friends, one of whom returned her to her home.'

'She found her husband dead. I didn't like to press the widow too hard for details when we met. What do we know of the circumstances?'

'Only what's been in the papers. Signs of entry through a ground-floor window. Winterton seems to have disturbed the thief in the upstairs sitting room and was hit, very hard, with the proverbial blunt instrument – possibly a brass book-end which was missing and, as far as I know, has yet to be found.'

'Do we know what else was stolen? Or did he flee in a panic?'

'That,' Mr Enterkin said, 'is why she wanted the inventory back. The only things which she was sure were missing were an antique gold watch and a pair of silver quaichs, both from the room where the body was found. Valuable, but not remarkably so. Presumably she is by now in a position to tell the police of anything else stolen.'

'Isn't that a bit odd?' Janet said. 'I mean, he entered downstairs but went straight up to a sitting room on the first floor.'

'It's not unusual,' Mr Enterkin said. 'Burglars often start upstairs where they're less likely to be interrupted and where the more portable valuables such as jewellery are probably to be found. Downstairs valuables tend to be heavier.'

'Right,' Keith said. 'Monday evening, Mrs Winterton returns and finds the body. Presumably she phones for the police, who spend Tuesday in feverish activity, searching for traces of the culprit, and then start looking for known thieves who could fit.

'By Wednesday afternoon, police activity at Halleydane House has died down. They'll still be very busy, but elsewhere. The widow, who seems to be a very strong-minded lady, has remained alone in the place. A knocker turns up and, unaware of the value of the collection, or so she says, she lets him take it away in exchange for a couple of hundred, cash. Whether he arrived by what was for him a happy chance, or followed up the news of the death, or was sent, we've no way of knowing at the moment.

'It seems that he'd been on the knock in that area for a couple of days beforehand. If it was the same chap,

Peter, you pinned him down as Duncan Laurie. I'd already arrived at Laurie by a different route so we can assume that we have the right man. Do we know of any other purchases than the ormolu clock?'

The baronet scratched his grey mop. 'Another clock,' he said. 'A tallcase, slightly damaged, the face painted with a scene of shepherds and milkmaids. He also came across a tulipwood games table which he very much wanted, but he didn't have the price on him in cash and the owner wasn't taking a cheque. He put down a deposit of a hundred pounds and promised to return.'

'That ties it up, then,' Keith said. 'Duncan Laurie was strapped for working capital. No knocker would work that way if he could possibly avoid it. The seller would almost certainly ask around and find out that he was being offered too little. Which means, of course, that Laurie would be easily tempted by any kind of a crooked deal. And I've seen the clock.'

'Where?' Janet asked.

'Be patient a little longer. All will be revealed. But if we jump around we'll miss something important. Nobody sold him a dower chest?'

'Not that they told me,' Sir Peter said. 'But I could only phone the larger and more likely places. If it came out of some semi with a few of great-granddad's pieces cluttering up the place, I wouldn't be likely to hear.'

'I suppose,' Mr Enterkin said, 'that you've had no response to the enquiries which my secretary made to the dealers?'

'Nothing,' Molly said.

'There was one odd coincidence,' said the solicitor. 'My secretary tells me that she was more than once met with the comment that a similar enquiry had been

54

received recently. They wanted to be assured that it was not the same enquiry arriving through different channels. She was able to reassure them.'

'Probably the original seller changed his or her mind,' Keith said. 'It might be worth going back to the dealers and finding out who made the earlier enquiry.

'We'll move on again. Thursday. Not much seemed to happen, except that I returned from my trip and got the news. Mrs Winterton confessed the error of her ways. And I asked you, Peter, to help identify the knocker who'd taken advantage of her folly and ignorance. So this morning, Friday, I went into Edinburgh for no better reasons than that it's the nearest big city and that Mrs Winterton's description of the man sounded as if he had an Edinburgh accent. I visited old Angus Pride. I wouldn't trust him further than I could spit an elephant, but he's a shrewd old devil and knows everything about everybody. We agreed that Duncan Laurie was the only Edinburgh-based knocker to fill the bill.

'If he'd bought the guns and hadn't already disposed of them, they'd be in his store in Waterman's Lane, so I went down there.'

'What about Michael Winterton?' Molly said.

'You're right, I'd forgotten. Michael, the late Mr Winterton's son, caught me outside Angus Pride's shop. He's another one who's strapped for capital. He hadn't much to say for himself except that he hoped I'd do what I could to settle the estate quickly. I pointed out that my hands were tied and that, in any case, he might not have anything coming.'

'He knew about his stepmother's stupidity then?' Mr Enterkin said.

'Yes. Family grape-vine, I suppose. I got rid of him

as quickly as I could and hared off down to Waterman's Lane. I got no answer at the door, which was unlocked, so I looked inside. And I found Duncan Laurie with his throat cut. It was meant to look like suicide but I don't believe it and the police, once they've had time to investigate, won't believe it either.'

Molly, who knew the story, sat quietly but the others produced a momentary babel of questions and comment. But they sat in rapt attention as Keith described the scene and outlined his few reasons for believing that Laurie had not died by his own hand.

'Some important points,' Keith went on, 'are these. One, there was a tallcase clock on the workbench with a painted dial which could well have shown a scene of shepherds and milkmaids, I didn't look too closely. Somebody had started work, repairing damage to the top of the case. Two, there was a dower chest not far from the body. And, three, I managed to sneak a look inside his pocket diary, which was on the desk in front of him. He only used it for reminders so it didn't tell me very much; but the only entry for Thursday referred to a D. Bruce.'

Keith paused.

'You can hardly be referring to the lady at the post office,' Mr Enterkin said at last. 'Nor yet to the actor of that name. You will have to enlighten us.'

'Think,' Keith said. 'It's not so very many years since we had dealings with a D. Bruce. He was the one man who could dispose of a unique collection obtained in dubious circumstances without making waves.'

'You mean Danny Bruce?' Molly squeaked. 'The antique-dealer.'

'And fence,' Sir Peter said thoughtfully. 'I recall that he was a fence in a big way of business before his

56

downfall. He's out, then?'

'Ages ago,' Keith said. 'And his daughter kept the Glasgow antique shops running while he was inside. I've no doubt he's been up to his old tricks long since.

'Under D. Bruce, the diary also said Rutherglen and then a scribble which might have been "Guns".

'"Dearie me," I said, "oh dearie, dearie me," or words to that effect.'

'I take it,' Mr Enterkin said, 'that you did not draw any of your conclusions to the attention of the police.'

'They'll get there soon enough,' Keith said. 'Meantime, the last thing I wanted was to get caught up in a murder enquiry and spend the rest of the day hanging around in case somebody thought of any more questions, while Danny Bruce was spiriting the guns away to hell and gone.

'So, as soon as I could get a moment's peace, I slipped away to the phone. I called his shop in Buchanan Street and Danny Bruce was there all right. I lowered the pitch of my voice and tried to put on an Aberdeen accent, and I said, "This is a friend. Don't try to get the guns away. The police know and they're watching for them." Then I hung up.'

'That'll just make him hide them away all the deeper,' Molly objected.

'Probably. But at least it should keep them in one place for a while,' Keith said. 'You remember what a cautious devil Danny was, always looking over his shoulder and jumping at shadows. He won't move them until he's absolutely sure that it's safe. Which gives me time to think what I'm going to do.'

'What are you going to do?' Janet asked.

'Pardon my French but I'm buggered if I know.'

'Pull the other one,' Janet said after a pause.

57

'I beg your pardon?' Keith said coldly.

'So you should,' said Molly.

'I can see why you wanted Sir Peter and Ralph here,' Janet persisted. 'But there's no obvious reason why you wanted Wal. I came instead of him and you haven't addressed a word to me. Therefore you wanted Wal to do something I wouldn't have approved of and now you're thinking you can phone him as soon as I've gone.'

'Everybody thinks they can read me like a book today,' Keith said.

'For years,' Janet said, 'you've been telling us to try and think like the other fellow, but you don't like it when we apply it to you. It works in business and it works in other ways too. Come on. What did you want Wal to do?'

Keith threw up his hands. 'All right,' he said. 'All bloody right. You'll all remember. Several years ago, we went chasing after two insurance company rewards.'

'We got them, too,' Molly said cheerfully. 'That's how we bought this house.'

'But Danny Bruce got in the way and instead of making a packet he got himself jugged. Even if I hadn't been doing business with him before that, he'd have had cause to remember me.

'What I wanted to do, and what I was going to suggest to Wal, was to go through, take a look at his shops and see if anything showed which could be traced back to Robin Winterton or to Duncan Laurie and maybe pretend to represent a rich customer busting to buy some of the collection and no questions asked.'

'No,' Janet said. 'Out of the question. Put it out of your tiny mind. Forget it. Find some other sucker.'

'Wal's the only one of us who came on the scene after

58

that particular event,' Keith pointed out. 'The rest of us were called at the trial.'

'Tough,' Janet said. 'My recollection of Danny Bruce is of a real smoothie with an icicle for a heart and a daughter who'd drop a grenade in a blind man's cup just for laughs. And neither of them went anywhere without one or more hard men for bodyguards. Wal's known to be your partner, and his stammer would make him easy to trace. No, thank you very much. Leave Wal out. Hire somebody who can't be traced back to us.'

'I get the message,' Keith said. 'You don't have to put it to music and sing it. Well, would you make a phone-call for me?'

'He's heard me on the phone.'

'You were using your Cheltenham-and-Girton voice. Be American. You're secretary to somebody you won't name over the phone but the cash is there. A pal tipped your boss off that there's maybe a couple of Scottish long guns coming on the alternative market and he'd like to bid.'

'Same answer,' Janet said. 'Get somebody else. Hire an actor.'

'I might do that,' Keith said. 'Or. . . . I wonder if one of the family would do it. They have the strongest incentive. Would Mrs Winterton's son be keen to redeem his mum's disastrous blunder?'

'I wouldn't go near him if I were you,' Molly said. 'I don't think he'd be your cup of tea at all. He used to turn up at some Camera Club meetings I went to in Edinburgh. His boy-friend was usually with him,' she finished, pink in the face.

'Oh,' Keith said. The prospect of trying to coax a homosexual had less than no appeal for him. He

59

changed tack. 'Janet, you remember Inspector Cathcart of Strathclyde, the one who took such pleasure in
arresting Danny Bruce at last?'

'Yes, of course.'

'He rather fancied you,' Keith said. 'Would you give
him a ring, renew old acquaintance? He owes us a
favour. He could pay it off by warning us if Danny
Bruce seems to be moving a heavy load around in a
secretive manner.'

'That much I'll do,' Janet said.

'Well, while you're on the phone. . . .' Keith set
about persuading Janet to call Danny Bruce. He could
usually twist her round his finger in the end.

When the visitors were gone, Keith settled down in the
study with the intention of making life very difficult for
anybody trying to dispose of Robin Winterton's collection.

Even after so many years largely spent trading in
antique guns, he was amazed to discover how many
potential buyers he could think of. Dealers, investors,
curators and collectors, they were all in his mind. He
knew how each worked and whether or not he was
honest. He knew whether a phone-call was enough or if
a letter would be necessary. He knew when to appeal
man-to-man and when to include a thinly-disguised
threat. His message was always the same: 'If you're
offered anything which might have come from the
Winterton collection, no matter how good the source or
the provenance seems to be, I want to know at once.'

He was interrupted once by an incoming phone-call.
He lifted the receiver quickly, hoping that it was news.

'This is Philip Stratton,' the caller said. 'You
remember me?'

It took a second or two for the name to evoke a tall, neatly-dressed figure topped by hair of purest silver. 'Reporter,' Keith said. 'The *Scotsman*. How are you doing?'

'Reasonably,' Stratton said. 'I left the *Scotsman*. I'm freelance now. I was tired of being told which stories to follow up and which to leave alone.'

That made sense. Philip Stratton had had a talent for investigative journalism. He might make a living as a freelance even in such a fiercely competitive profession. 'I wish you luck,' Keith said.

'You can do a little more than that – you can feed me a story. I heard a whisper that you were the executor of the Robin Winterton who was killed during a robbery a few days ago.'

'True,' Keith said.

'Today, things being quiet, I was doing the rounds of the police stations and your name pops up again, this time as the finder of an apparent suicide, although the police are being a bit cagey as to whether they're treating it as such. An antique-dealer.'

'Also true.'

'What's the connection?'

Keith thought quickly. The press would have the whole story all too soon, but for the moment he would not want that sort of publicity alerting every petty crook and con-man. 'I've no comment to make,' he said. 'But give me your number. I may have something for you in a day or two.'

FOUR

Molly was downstairs ahead of her family in the morning but, before she could take her breakfast, Keith had followed her down and was scrambling through his own meal as if it might be his last. Within five minutes he was only anchored to the table by his second cup of coffee and by the fact that he was still lacing his shoes.

'What's the hurry?' Molly demanded. 'Aren't you waiting for Deborah?'

'You really want me to take her along? I nearly walked her into a pool of blood yesterday. I'm going through to Glasgow. See what the Strathclyde fuzz have dug up and take a look at Danny Bruce's shops for myself.'

'Well, don't drive too fast. If you're in such a hurry—'

'I've plenty of time to get to Glasgow,' Keith said. 'I'm just in a hurry to get out of here. Unless the Edinburgh force is slacker than I think it is, they've spotted by now that Duncan Laurie was tweeped—'

'Was what?'

'Terminated with Extreme Prejudice. That's what they call it in the upper-underworld. They'll have found "D. Bruce" in his diary. I couldn't point out the connection without admitting I'd been poking through the clues before they got there, which is enough to put any hidebound copper's back up. But Strathclyde will have told them about my enquiry by now. So they'll see that there was a connection after all and they'll be wondering whether mine was an inspired guess or whether I know something they don't. And any minute now there'll be a posse at the door, wanting to keep me hanging around making statements until the cows come home.'

Before Molly could speak, the front door bell, right on its cue, chimed in the hall.

'Too late,' Keith said with a sigh. 'Would you give me a minute and then bring them to the study? Then listen at the hatch.' The trunk of a former dumb-waiter led down from the study to the basement. 'And listen carefully. I may want a witness to what I really said.'

Before settling, Keith stole a glance from the study window. A fawn Granada stood on the gravel. Two men occupied the front seats and Keith could hear voices at the front door. A large party, then. He sat down at his desk and began to scribble on a sheet of paper, playing the part of the solid businessman being interrupted by unwelcome public servants.

The door opened. 'Mrs Anguillas,' Molly's voice said, in the tone which she used to announce that the puppy had made a mess on the carpet. Keith was puzzled. He knew nobody of that name.

Mary Bruce rounded the corner and came into the room.

As he rose to his feet, Keith nodded to himself. Now

he understood. Before his marriage, he had had an affair with Mary Bruce. Less forgivably, it had been renewed on one short but pleasant later occasion. Molly suspected both these facts but without, he thought, being quite sure of them. Whatever they got up to now, he thought with inner amusement, they had better keep the conversation going.

'Mary!' he said. 'How nice to see you again! Do sit down and forgive me if I finish what I was doing. Hang on, Molly. This is urgent. Would you type it up and get it away, please?'

Molly waited. She was too wise to comment. Keith did all his own typing.

As if continuing his draft Keith wrote, 'Phone your brother, get him to follow when she leaves. Fawn Granada outside with two men. Are they staying locally? Who do they see?' He gave it to Molly who scanned it briefly, nodded and withdrew.

Keith returned his attention to Mary Bruce – Mary Anguillas, he must now learn to say. 'I heard that you'd entered Holy Bedlock,' he said, 'but nobody told me your new name.'

She smiled. She was older and her face had changed, losing most of what little beauty it had ever had, but she had looked after her figure and she retained more than her share of animal magnetism. 'It was never intended to be a permanent arrangement,' she said. 'But while the heat was on – thanks to you – dual nationality had a lot to be said for it. How are things with yourself? Is that little wife of yours keeping you at peace with the world?'

Keith hoped very much that Molly was engaged on the phone. 'I'm content,' he said. 'But I'm sure you didn't come all this way to enquire after my sex-life.'

64

She laughed coarsely. 'Are you? There was a time you might have hoped that I had. But no, Keith. This is a normal business visit.' She looked him in the eyes. 'Following up your phone-calls.'

He tried to keep from showing concern, but he knew how much his eyes must be giving away. 'What phone-calls?'

Mary modestly pulled her skirt down, thereby drawing his attention to her wholly admirable legs. 'Dad was sitting quietly in one of the shops yesterday when the phone rang and a badly-disguised voice advised him not to try to move "the guns" because the police were taking an interest. It meant nothing to him at first, because any guns which have been through the shops lately have been legit and in ones and pairs. But mention of guns made him remember you, and he decided that the voice could have been yours and you always did have a penchant for tricky phone-calls. And he remembered seeing Old Man Winterton's death in the papers and hearing a whisper that you were his executor. So he starts phoning round friends in the trade. And he picks up a rumour that there was something very special in Winterton's collection and that you're running around in a flap because some knocker conned the widow into unloading the whole lot for a few quid. Well, Keith?'

'No comment,' Keith said.

'He also hears that Duncan Laurie was found with his throat cut. You wouldn't have done that, would you, Keith?'

'Good God, no!' Keith said explosively. 'When did I ever use violence?'

'You want a list?'

Thinking back, Keith realised that he had from time

65

to time been involved – defensively, of course – in violent clashes. 'I didn't kill Duncan Laurie,' he said. 'In fact, I found him yesterday morning and I called the police straight away.'

'You must have changed. How long had he been dead?'

'You know that even a trained pathologist'll jib at telling you that. Long enough to give me an alibi, anyway.'

'Make a guess.'

Keith thought about it and could see no harm in divulging what would be in the papers soon enough. 'I'm only guessing. But from the congealing of the blood I'd think the evening before. Give or take a couple of days, if I only had the blood to go by.'

'I see. . . . Later, another voice phoned, a woman this time, to say that she had a customer for the guns. That was one of your cronies, of course. And a very good friend tells us that the Strathclyde police have been tipped off that we might be moving some incriminating goodies abroad. You again, of course, and not very friendly.'

'You're jumping to a hell of a lot of conclusions,' Keith said.

'If I'm wrong, if you're not interested, just say so.' Keith remained silent. 'So, if Dad should by any chance get a clue to where those guns are, you'd be interested?'

'I am not buying them back,' Keith said hotly. 'The widow had no right to sell them, so there can be no valid title. I suppose I'd be justified in offering a finder's fee.'

'Ten per cent of the realised value?' She had lowered her lids but was watching him intently.

66

'Hold your horses,' Keith said. 'Switch off that greedy gleam in your eye. That could be a hell of a lot of money.'

'Which means that the collection's worth ten times as much,' she said.

'But every one of those guns – the valuable ones, anyway – is individual. If they come on the market at any time, I'll know. And if I can track them back to your old man, he goes inside again.'

'I doubt it.'

'Believe me. Because he could hardly come by those guns without linking himself with Duncan Laurie's death. Five per cent, and he'd be doing very nicely. Provided that the collection's complete. I'm not having him sell off the commoner items and claim a finder's fee on the unique ones.'

She nodded and he knew that they could have a firm agreement, if they cared to abide by it. 'But this is pie in the sky,' she said. 'What I really came to say was that there's some good stuff in Halleydane House. If it's coming on the market, Dad would like a chance to offer.'

'It'll probably be auctioned,' Keith said.

'Suit yourself. If the dealers make a ring, he can probably get what he wants cheaper.' She relaxed in her chair and looked around the room. 'You've come up in the world since you were living and dealing in the back of a converted bank-van. I hear you bought this place with the rewards you got, you know when.'

'It helped,' Keith admitted.

'No hard feelings. Not a lot, anyway.' She nudged the front of his desk with her toe. 'If your doing so well, it's time you traded some of these fakes for the real thing.'

'They're not fakes,' Keith said hotly, 'they're repro-
ductions.'

'Same difference. Dad handles a lot of good stuff
these days. Play ball and he could give you a good
trade.' She looked at her watch. Diamonds sparked in
the light. 'And now I'd better be going, or the boys will
think you've decided to tie me up and torture me.'

'I won't bother,' Keith said. 'You'd probably enjoy
it.'

'Make me an offer I can't refuse,' she said lightly.
She got up to go, smoothing her skirt down over her
perfect hips. 'And don't forget what I've said.'

'I'll remember what you said,' Keith promised, 'as
well as what you didn't say.'

Keith returned from the front door and met Molly in
the kitchen. 'Anything left in the coffee-pot?' he asked.

Molly filled a mug for him and sat down opposite.
'You're not still in a hurry, then?'

'There's no brattle now. Unless that whole thing was
a bluff to put me off while they got the guns out of the
country. What did you think?'

'What did you?' Molly retorted. 'I couldn't see her
face, such as it is.'

'Her face wasn't giving anything away, except her
age. If Danny's got the guns, he knew about them
beforehand. He's ready to deal, but Duncan Laurie's
death's turned the heat on. He'll maybe make me an
offer later on – if I didn't push too hard, offer too little.'

'And if he hasn't got them?'

Keith was staring into space. Molly waited patiently.
'In that case,' he said at last, 'I probably said too much.'

'Which do you think it is? You must have some idea.'

'Or else Danny was supposed to get them and they've

gone adrift because somebody killed Duncan Laurie for
them. Which would have to be somebody who knew
their value. I think. . . . on balance, I think he's got
them. Did you get hold of Ronnie?'

'He was just leaving his house, but I caught him. He
said he'd come straight away. He'll do what he can.'

'If he can tell me what Mary and her little lambs do
next, that should give us a lead. If they try to follow me
around, I'll know they haven't got the guns but they've
come through on spec to try and grab them. I only hope
Ronnie got here in time. I couldn't keep her talking any
longer – she'd have become suspicious. Those Bruces
have a sixth sense for deviousness, being so damn
devious themselves.'

'He must have been here in time,' Molly said. 'I sent
Deborah to meet him at the road. She'd have come
back if he'd missed them.'

'You what?' Keith said loudly.

'She came downstairs while I was phoning and
wanted to go with Ronnie. I thought it might be helpful
if somebody was at the main road to see which way they
turned, in case Ronnie just missed them, so I shot some
breakfast into her and sent her out. She'll be all right
with Ronnie.'

'Sometimes I wonder about you,' Keith said. 'You
get up to high doh if I let her out of my sight for a few
seconds in a crowded street to buy shoes and then you
send her off to wait on a deserted country road for yon
daft brother of yours when he's trying to shadow Mary
Bruce and two of her father's hard men. Suppose they
realise they're being followed and try to run Ronnie off
the road?'

'Ronnie'll be in his Land-Rover,' Molly said. 'I don't
see anybody running him off the road very easily.'

Keith could see the logic of her argument. If anybody was run off the road, Ronnie was more likely to be the aggressor. 'They'd need a tank. All the same,' he said, 'suppose she's out of the car for a moment and Ronnie sees his quarry drive off. What's he going to do? Leave her behind?'

For the first time, Molly looked anxious. 'I hope he wouldn't do that,' she said.

'I hope he would,' Keith said. 'This is important.' He laughed suddenly. 'Fancy Mary Bruce turning up again, after all these years.'

'Do you?' Molly asked in a small voice.

Keith blinked at her. 'Do I what?'

'Fancy Mary Bruce. You used to. . . .' She got up and came round the table to put an arm round his shoulders. 'You don't still find her attractive, do you?'

'Do you know,' Keith said, 'I never saw the two of you at the same time before. As far as sexually attractive goes, it was like seeing a pair of lace briefs beside a panty-girdle.'

'Oh yes? And which was I?' Molly asked.

'You know which you were,' Keith said. He gave her bottom a reassuring pat and realised to his dismay that she was wearing a panty-girdle.

There was no point now in trailing away to Glasgow. On the other hand, even if Keith had known where his brother-in-law and his daughter were being led, he would have been more of a hindrance than a help in following Mary Bruce and her helpers. If Mary had done her homework with her usual thoroughness, his cars would be as well known as his face while, as far as he could remember, Mary had never set eyes on Molly's brother, and Land-Rovers displaying mud over

70

the original green were a common sight on the local roads.

Keith decided to go in search of background. When you don't know what facts you want, get what facts you can, he told himself.

Although the Calders were now a two-car family, there was the usual tussle over cars. Keith had been unanimous in deciding that the second car would be one of the new Japanese jeep-type vehicles, ideally suited for use on shooting days. Molly had tried it once and, having changed into four-wheel-drive by mistake and signalled several times with the wipers, refused to drive it again. Keith argued that the hatchback was more suitable for the longer run on good roads but he lost the argument. Molly had shopping to do and that was that.

Keith consulted the telephone directory and a map and set off, steeling himself to ignore the stiff suspension and higher noise-level.

The Winterton family, and in particular their financial affairs, would stand some looking into. He had already met Robin Winterton's widow and his son, but the stepson, Steven Clune, he had only glimpsed in passing. Reluctantly, because Keith was nervous of homosexuals, he left the main road at Soutra and headed towards Haddington. The only Clune S. in the phone-book lived near North Berwick.

He crossed the A1 and continued north towards the Firth of Forth. He made two turns in accordance with his patchy recollection, and had just decided to stop and refresh his memory of the map when he saw roofs ahead and the spire of a small church.

Then he braked hard and, because the jeep had ferocious brakes, nearly hit his nose on the windscreen.

71

Ronnie's ox-like figure was out in the road and waving his arms and Keith saw the Land-Rover pulled tight against the hedge and his daughter's head at the window. He pulled in behind the Land-Rover and got out. A curve in the road hid them from the village.

'What's up?'

'It's lucky yon wee bizzum's observant,' Ronnie said. 'They've stopped round the corner at the first wee house. If she'd not seen you coming you'd've run on to them. Get in the Land-Rover and you'll see the place.'

Keith climbed in beside his daughter. Through the windscreen and a gap in the hedge he could see across a field of barley stubble to a post-war bungalow, painted in pastel colours. The Granada was pulled on to the verge, pointing away from them.

'They came straight here?' Keith asked.

'Except for a stop at a phone-box. Got here about twenty minutes back.'

'And you'd no trouble?'

Ronnie's craggy face screwed up. 'I wouldna' say that. There was aye some other traffic I could hide in, but I'd a job to keep up. They fairly flew.'

Deborah nodded vigorously. 'So did we,' she said. 'I didn't know a Land-Rover could go so fast.'

'Nor me,' Ronnie said. 'The Land-Rover didn't know it either.'

'Well, you ken fine now,' Keith said. 'When they leave, you follow them again. Deborah can bide with me. I'll try to find out what they were after. When you can, phone Molly to say where you are. And, Ronnie, you have a gun with you?'

'Not a shotgun. Just rifles.' Ronnie was by profession a stalker.

'That'll do. Stay well out of the way unless they seem

72

to be loading a lot of stuff into the car.'

'And if they do?'

'Stop them,' Keith said. 'Any way you like.'

Ronnie nodded grimly and Keith was satisfied. Whatever attributes Ronnie might lack, he had not been hiding behind the door when ruthlessness and grit were handed out.

'They're more likely to drive on and circle back to the main road,' Keith said, 'but if they turn back this way, keep your head right down out of sight.'

'I wish I knew what the hell's going on,' Ronnie said plaintively. 'Molly said she'd no time to tell me a damned thing and Deb says you swore her to secrecy.'

'See me tonight and I'll fill you in. For the moment, just believe that it's important.'

'Something's happening,' Deborah said.

Mary Bruce came out of the bungalow followed by two men – the two, Keith presumed, who had earlier been sitting in the car. As far as Keith could judge at a range of a hundred yards, they seemed pleased with themselves. One of the men was carrying a polythene bag which held something brown. It seemed to weigh lightly – if it contained guns it could only have held a pistol or two. They got into the Granada and drove away.

Keith and Deborah climbed down and got into the jeep. Ronnie drove off in a hurry and they followed more slowly. Keith pulled up in front of the bungalow. He thought about leaving Deborah in the jeep but decided that the Bruce party might return. Anyway, it was none too soon for her to learn a few more facts of life. 'You'd better come with me, Toots,' he said.

The bungalow was expensively finished with a stone front and hardwood windows, double-glazed. A double garage stood open and the car which he had seen in Newton Lauder's square was looking out at them. The bungalow's front door, of teak, was slightly ajar.

Keith was about to press the bell-push beside the door when a sound from inside made him pause. Somebody was groaning, regularly, with each outgoing breath. The sound was piteous and he felt the hair crawl up the back of his neck.

Without stopping to think, he pushed the door open and went inside. The hallway was deeply carpeted and, despite the terracotta and moss-green paint, there was light enough to see that it was hung with prints of Aubrey Beardsley's quite shocking illustrations to *Lysistrata*. Steven Clune, it appeared, was not hiding in any closet. Keith turned to send Deborah outside but she had already followed the sounds through another open door and into a living room made exotic by satins and by an expensive oriental wallpaper which, when looked into, revealed a distinctly erotic theme.

A man was lying on his side, his hands tied behind him. Keith recognised the face as belonging to Steven Clune, assuming that it had been Clune who had collected his mother after the meeting in Mr Enterkin's office. It was less pretty than when Keith had last seen it, being disfigured by several lumps and stained with blood. Keith was relieved to note that most of this had come from a nose which appeared to be broken. His body showed the welts and bruises of a thorough beating.

Clune had been wearing a silk dressing-gown but this was now up around his shoulders. His body was nude. Well, Keith thought with a sidelong glance at Deborah, that at least could have been worse. He bent down and pulled as much of the silk robe as he could gather over

74

the man's nakedness.

For the first time, Clune became aware of somebody else outside of his personal cocoon of misery. He jumped and uttered a strangled sound which Keith interpreted as 'No more'.

'Relax,' Keith said. 'I'm not an enemy.' He tried to untie the other's wrists but the many turns of fishing-line defeated him. He reached behind him for the knife in the sheath taped across the back of his belt, at the same time speaking over his shoulder to Deborah. 'Find the phone. Call the police and an ambulance.'

'No.' Clune spat out a tooth. His voice was slightly stronger. 'Nobody else.'

Keith finished cutting the bonds and helped Clune to bring his upper arm round to the front. Clune relaxed, half on his face. He seemed prepared to wait there until the pain went away.

'Any bones broken?' Keith asked.

'Don't . . . think . . . so.'

'Can you wiggle your toes?' He saw Clune's toes move. 'Any stabbing pains when you breathe?'

Clune breathed noisily through his mouth for a few seconds. 'Not what you'd call stabbing,' he said faintly.

'Then I guess it's safe for you to move. Deborah, see if you can find the kitchen. Bring a bowl of very cold water and a soft cloth. Now, laddie, let's get you on to the settee.'

'Don't want . . . bleed on to the upholstery. It's new. And it cost . . .'

'Only your nose seems to have been bleeding and it's stopped.'

'Right.' With Keith's help, Steven Clune got as far as a sitting position and then stopped. 'No police,' he said again. 'And no ambulance.'

75

'Your nose is broken. You'll have to have it set.'
'I'll get my own doctor. Will it hurt?'
'Not a lot.'
'Dear God! And I've messed the carpet.'
'Only a fcw spots of blood,' Keith said comfortingly, as if to a child. 'We'll soak them in cold water. Give them a wash in salt water later. They'll come out.' Keith had had a rough youth and was not inexperienced with bloodstains.

When Deborah came back, carrying with great care a bowl of black Wedgwood and a soft duster, Clune was on the settee, his dressing-gown more modestly disposed about his person.

'Well done,' Keith said. 'Now, hot, sweet tea. I'll come and get you started.' She showed him the kitchen, a bright, clean room which did not seem to lack the feminine touch. 'Go through the place,' Keith said urgently. 'See if there's any sign of those guns. Don't bother about places which could only take pistols, it's the Scottish long guns we're after. Don't miss any sheds.'

'All right, Dad.' She was as eager as a pup in training. This was the first time that she had been allowed an active part in one of Keith's more adventurous undertakings.

While Deborah was left to follow his instructions, Keith got on with cleaning up Steven Clune and applying cold compresses to the worst of the bruises. If he had remembered that the body under his ministration belonged to a homosexual he would probably have turned away in revulsion; but from outside it seemed such a normal body that the thought never entered his head, although he did pause to wonder what on God's earth Deborah might be finding. Well, as long as she didn't tell her mother. . .

'What were they after?' he asked suddenly.

It took Clune a few moments to gather his wits and bring his mind back from his own miseries and the condition of the furniture. Then realisation hit him. He stared in horror at a comparatively innocent photograph of *The Boy David*. 'Oh my God!' he said. 'What have I done?'

'Tell me, then.'

'I can't.' Clune lowered his face into his hands. It took several tries before he could find unbruised areas to support.

'What did they take away?'

'Nothing! I can't tell you! Leave me alone!' Clune's voice began to rise hysterically.

'Don't get your . . .' Keith paused. He had been about to use an expression which, in the context, would have been less than tactful – '. . . bowels in an uproar,' he substituted. 'It can't be that bad.'

'It is.' Clune raised a face which Keith saw was now marked with tears. 'It's awful. It's the worst thing that could have happened. And it's my fault.'

'What is?'

'I can't tell you. Please, stop asking me.'

'You told them.'

'That was different. You can't imagine how terrible they were. I can't stand physical pain. I told them all they wanted to know almost straight away. And – would you believe? – they went on beating me up anyway, not bothering to ask any questions. And calling me names.' Clune was sobbing now, like a child, not attempting to hide his tears.

Keith decided to approach from another direction. 'Did they know exactly what they were after?'

Clune's sobs broke off while he thought about it. 'No,' he said at last. 'They'd guessed or heard that there was something. They just started bashing me and telling me I'd better come up with what I'd . . . Never mind. And – oh Jesus Christ! – I told them the whole thing.'

Faintly, Keith heard the sound of a loft-ladder being pulled down. He spoke up to cover the noise. 'You told them where the guns are?'

'I don't know anything about guns. This was far worse. What have I done?' he wailed. 'It was nothing much when it started. But now . . .'

Keith was getting lost. 'You know that your mother—'

'The old bitch! This is all her fault,' Clune said petulantly. 'I hope it costs her.'

'Her fault? For selling the guns?'

'No, no, no. For . . . for . . . oh, never mind! For what I did. You wouldn't understand.'

'Try me.'

'No. I can't tell anybody. That's what makes it awful. And there's no way I can stop it happening.'

'I may be able to stop it,' Keith said hopefully. 'Once they'd got what they wanted out of you, whatever it was, where would they go next?'

'To . . . to my stepbrother, I suppose.'

'Would he be in any danger?'

'I don't know. It would depend what he . . . I'm not going to tell you any more.' Clune looked up as Deborah came in and he struggled to recapture some shreds of dignity. His sobs had already subsided to hiccups. 'You've been very kind, but please go.'

Deborah put down a tray with a teapot, cup, sugar, milk and biscuits on an ornate coffee-table. She gave

78

her father a surreptitious headshake.

'Can you manage now?' Keith asked.

'I'll be all right,' Clune said. 'I can always phone Bobby to come home if I need him. He went in to open the shop. Fabrics, you know. But our customers are mostly trade, so Saturday's very quiet.'

'Will your stepbrother be at home?'

'Probably not. He might be at the surgery. He's a vet and they're busy on Saturdays.'

Keith considered sending Deborah away and extracting the information from Clune by the method which the earlier visitors had found so effective. But he could not bring himself to inflict pain on so abject a creature. 'We'll go now,' he said. 'You'd better phone your stepbrother and warn him not to be caught alone. If you decide to tell me any more, here's my card.'

'I won't,' Clune said. 'But thanks.' He seemed to be speaking only to Deborah. 'I'm sorry you had to see me like that. I'm not usually a total coward but you can't believe how awful they were, beating me for fun and accusing me of spreading that awful new disease. And we're no more promiscuous than anybody else. Probably less.'

'It's all right,' Deborah said. She kissed Clune at the side of the mouth. Keith got her out of there in a hurry.

FIVE

Rather than use Steven Clune's phone, Keith set off but stopped at the first phone-box to call Molly. Ronnie had already phoned her. His quarry had stopped for lunch at Dalkeith.

That ruled out a visit to Michael Winterton, who lived and practised near Dunbar. On the other hand, Dalkeith was on the shortest route to Halleydane House which stood in open country near Penicuik. Keith set off in pursuit and wound the low-geared jeep up to a frenzied 70 m.p.h. when the road allowed.

He raised his voice to be heard. 'You're sure you couldn't have missed them?'

'Positive.' Her higher voice penetrated the rush of sound from the speeding engine, off-the-road tyres and the wind. 'I looked everywhere. The attic—'

'I heard you.'

'—the sheds, under the beds and in the wardrobes.'

'Oh.' Keith tried to forget the implications. 'What about under the floorboards?'

Deborah adopted her most patronising tone, the one which made her parents want to slap her. 'There aren't any floorboards,' she said. 'It's all parquet flooring and solid. I think it's on concrete.'

'I think you're right.'

A few miles went by before Deborah said, 'Mr Clune's queer, isn't he?'

Keith felt his ears go hot. 'How do you mean?'

'Gay,' Deborah said. 'A poof.' The fact that she had almost to shout made the words on her lips the more shocking.

'What do you know about such things?'

'Quite a lot. Kirstie's brother's queer.'

'I didn't know that,' Keith said. He stayed calm with an effort. Kirstie was Deborah's bosom friend. 'Are you sure?'

'Absolutely. He can't let on to his parents until he leaves home. But he's quite open with us. We buy clothes for him sometimes, when he has the money. But I think it's sad. I try to let him see that girls aren't enemies. Don't tell Mum,' Deborah added. 'She'd be shocked.'

'I bet she would. Even I'm shocked. Knowing . . . what you know, you kissed Steven Clune!'

'Why not? He needed comforting.'

'Not from you.'

'He liked it,' Deborah said. She sounded confident.

'Am I coming on like a heavy father?'

He heard her clear laugh. 'A bit. But you don't often, so I'll forgive you.'

Thinking back to Kirstie's brother, it occurred to Keith that Deborah, at her present stage of development, was a tomboy, almost half boy. A boy who was half girl would only be meeting her halfway. He had not been looking forward to the day when he would have to explain homosexuality to Deborah. It now seemed that

81

she was better placed to explain such things to him.

Keith admitted to himself that, like most parents, he often thought of Deborah as she had been as a child and not as she now was, an incipient woman. She had her own friends but, being an only child, perforce spent much time in adult company.

'Do you ever feel that we're robbing you of your childhood?' he asked.

'That old thing!' Deborah said. 'I'll make you a present of it.'

Keith was suddenly conscious of the passing years, a subject which he usually avoided except when the occasional twinge of stiffness forced it on his attention. One of these days, she would make him a grandfather. He found it impossible to think of himself in that light. They passed Dalkeith in comparative silence.

Returning to present problems, Keith decided that he had been playing his cards too close to his chest. There was no reason to be secretive. The more people knew the better. What he needed was an army of inquisitive observers who would maintain such a watch that no surreptitious movement of the guns would be possible.

Mention, by Molly, of lunch had reminded him that he was hungry.

In Eskbank, he stopped for a few minutes. While Deborah visited a 'carry-out', he phoned Philip Stratton. When they drove on, Deborah was feeding him scampi and chips and giving him drinks from a screwtop of lemonade.

Halleydane House was a slightly larger version of the Calders' home at Briesland House – a substantial early Victorian dwelling, built as the hub of a small estate but now separated from most of its lands. Beyond the stone pillars in the boundary wall, a quarter of a mile of drive, lined with rhododendrons and shaded by mature trees, insulated the house from the passing traffic. The house and its gardens were surrounded by more trees, rhododendrons, azaleas and a variety of other shrubs of which Keith could have named only half.

Only careful observation of the verge for tyre-marks enabled Keith to track down the deserted Land-Rover deep in the bushes, but he found his brother-in-law comfortably established under a conifer on the far side of the strip of jungle bordering the drive, seated with his back against the trunk. Ronnie had binoculars in his hand, a rifle across his knees and a box of beer-cans nearby. Keith and Deborah squatted beside him and Keith accepted a can of lager.

Their position looked across a field or paddock and an acre of lawns to the corner of the house. The Granada stood on the left, under the pair of large rowan trees which sheltered the house's front door from the north wind. To the right was the garden front of the house containing most of the principal windows. The arrangement, Keith was pleased to note, was architecturally less satisfying than that of Briesland House.

'They only got here a half-hour since,' Ronnie said. 'One of the men took a walk round the house just now, otherwise nothing.'

Keith pondered. He would have liked to have waited for further developments. But Mary Bruce and her friends might be giving the widow a rough time and, while he had no great liking for the autocratic lady, he could hardly leave her at their mercy.

But a few more minutes would be neither here nor

there. He gave Molly's brother a quick summary of what had gone before.

Inevitably, Ronnie had picked up from Keith some knowledge of antique guns and their values. His eyes widened. 'An' you offered they buggers five per cent of a' that. You must bc dottled!'

'I'd no intention of paying it,' Keith said indignantly. 'I mentioned the figure as a come-on. Trouble is, I think she guessed. So if she comes by the collection, she'll go elsewhere or offer the guns back to me at a figure the estate'll have to pay.'

'Sounds to me,' Ronnie said, 'as if there was a fiddle set up between Danny Bruce and the family and it went wrong. Danny Bruce sent yon dealer mannie to buy the stuff, for much more than the figure she owned up to, but the widow cheated on him somehow. He had the dealer put down and now he's after what he's paid for.'

'Could be. But I don't get that feeling. Danny Bruce never used to set out to be violent. And I can't see what the family stood to gain. The money from the guns was coming to them anyway and the capital transfer tax would have been no more than Danny Bruce would expect for his cut. I think I'll go in and give Mary a surprise.'

'I don't blame you,' Ronnie said with a wink hidden from Deborah. He had always rather fancied Mary Bruce himself.

'She's got two very hard boys with her,' Keith pointed out. 'And they've just given Steven Clune a damn good beating. Just in case they think to do the same to me, I want some back-up. You two bide here. If you see me signal from outside the door or wave a handkerchief at a window, fire a shot. Don't hit me,' he said firmly, 'but let there be no doubt that I've got friends out here with live ammunition. If they carry a heavy load out to the car, don't let them leave. But if all's peaceful and they've put nothing into the car, let them go by and see if you can follow them again. If they head for Glasgow, let them go and meet me back here. If not, I'd like to know where they are. Got that?'

'Aye,' Ronnie said. 'And Deborah?'

'Better take her with you.'

Keith drove the jeep up to the front door. Well-maintained grass bordered the last of the narrow, tarmac drive. He would have preferred the open, if only to avoid the careless defecation of the birds, but to park on the grass would surely have incurred more of the widow's displeasure and he could imagine circumstances in which he would prefer Mary Bruce to make an unimpeded departure. He drove on to the gravel sweep under the spread of the rowan trees and parked beside the Granada.

He was not looking forward to a confrontation with a violent group while he had only the vaguest idea of his own objectives, but he had no time to develop doubts. The front door, in its formal, arched portico and flanked with beds of berberis blazing with berries, opened as he walked up to it. One of the men whom he had seen in Mary Bruce's car came out. The man was large, well-built and blond. His mouth and chin were weak, but he had the aggressive confidence of the habitual tough, born out of training or armament or both.

'Mrs Winterton is not receiving visitors,' he said, formally but with an air of amusement. He then spoiled the effect by adding, 'Fuck off.'

'I'm not a visitor,' Keith said. 'I'm the executor of

85

her husband's estate and this house is part of it. You fuck off.'

'You're Calder, are you? Well, today isn't convenient. You're not coming in.'

'You're wrong, Sonny Jim,' Keith said. 'In is exactly where I'm coming. Try and stop me.'

He was ready for a punch, but the man brought his right hand out from behind his leg holding a long-barrelled revolver, a copy, probably Belgian Keith thought, of the Smith and Wesson Russian model, and put it against Keith's chest.

Keith wanted that pistol in his own fist before he went any further. He held the man's eyes. 'My friends know I'm here. And they know you're here. Are you really going to let that thing off?'

While he spoke, and without looking down again, he stroked one finger of his left hand along the eight-inch barrel of the revolver. The hammer was already cocked, which negated the possibility of gripping the cylinder to prevent any movement of the action. Instead, Keith slipped his thumb under the hammer and then took a firm grip.

To Keith's surprise and probably his own, the man pulled the trigger. The hammer pinched Keith's thumb, not very painfully.

Keith was wide open to a punch from the man's left hand. But in more ways than one a man with a gun is at a disadvantage. The gun conveys power and generates over-confidence, while its user concentrates his mind on it and forgets other forms of attack. By the time the man took his mind off the revolver's inexplicable refusal to function, Keith had taken a handful of male glands in his right hand and squeezed. The man went up on his toes, his eyes crossed and he let go of the

86

revolver in order to grip Keith's wrist with both hands. But he still had sense enough not to pull.

Wondering if he hadn't caught a bear by the tail, Keith tried to juggle the revolver with his left hand, but he could not pull his thumb free one-handed without a shot being fired.

'What the hell . . .?' Another man had appeared from the direction of the drawing room, a smaller man, darker, with what Keith thought of as Jewish features and a hare-lip. Without hesitating, he ran at Keith, hands out as if to grip his lapels. Just in time, Keith recognised the signs, the stiffened neck-muscles and unfocusing eyes, and he lowered his own head before the butt to his face could land. Instead, he felt the other's nose smack down on to the crown of his own head.

His first opponent was emitting a high, hissing sound and Keith realised that the later flurry of movement had been transmitted through his handhold. He released the man and pushed him away. The smaller man was moaning and holding his face. Keith freed his left thumb from under the revolver's hammer and then, carefully holding back the hammer with his other thumb, used the barrel to administer a sharp rap on the skull to each man. The darker man went down, bleeding copiously from the nose over the hare-lip. The taller, fair man stayed on his feet. Keith had neither the time nor the means to assess whether he were still a danger, so he swept his leg round and kicked the man's feet out from under him. The man dropped heavily into a sitting position and rolled over.

'Here endeth the first lesson. That,' Keith said, 'was for beating up harmless poofs. The second lesson will be for fun.'

Without awaiting an answer, he walked through the open door of the drawing room. His heart was beating hard, his mouth was dry and he could feel his knees shaking.

The spacious drawing room was almost uncomfortably warm. Although the room was equipped with radiators the central heating did not seem to be on, but Mrs Winterton and Mary Bruce were seated comfortably on either side of an Adam fireplace in which an unnecessary log fire was smouldering. If there had been tea or sherry on the occasional table it would have been a cosy scene.

Mary's eyes flicked to the bone-handled revolver in Keith's hand. 'What was all that fuss about?' she asked.

'One of your goons pulled a gun,' Keith said. 'You may remember that I spend my life around guns. It's against my religion to have them pointed at me.'

'Eric always was impetuous,' Mary said. The remark implied that Eric had had the only firearm. But, Keith wondered, was this a snare? Mary had always been the tricky one.

Keith took an upright chair which had its back to the wall. 'If he's in the habit of producing guns at the drop of a hat,' he said, 'you'd better buy him something better than this.'

'What's wrong with it?'

Watching Mary out of the corner of his eye, Keith opened the revolver and looked at the proof-marks. 'Made in a Belgian back-street and sold in a Glasgow pub for a fiver or two. No rebounding lock, just a half-cock position which I wouldn't trust inside a glass case. And it must weigh over a kilo. No,' Keith added quickly, snapping the revolver shut, 'keep your hand away from your handbag. I'm sure you've got something better there but I don't want to see it just now.' He raised the muzzle of the revolver an inch.

Mrs Winterton had been looking at him much as she would have regarded a flasher at a garden-party. 'How dare you come bursting in here in this violent way?' she demanded. 'By what right?'

'I came,' Keith said, 'in case you were in any danger. These people have just given that son of yours a thorough battering.'

She seemed unmoved by the news, as if it were either stale or uninteresting, he could not be sure which. 'Steven brings these things on himself.'

'Perhaps,' Keith said. 'What reason did they give you for their visit?'

The older woman looked at the younger. 'We came,' Mary said quickly, 'to tell Mrs Winterton that a man had sold this to one of my father's shops yesterday afternoon.' She picked up a silver table-lighter which Keith had supposed to belong on the table beside her. 'We thought that it might have been taken at the time of the . . . burglary.'

'Why did that make it necessary to beat up Steven Clune?' Keith asked.

'We didn't want to bother Mrs Winterton in her time of bereavement,' Mary said. 'So we visited her son. But my companions took offence at some of his remarks.'

Keith shrugged off the obviousness of the lie. But what was behind it? 'Do you have a description of the man?' he asked.

'A young man, roughly spoken, wearing jeans,' Mary said. 'The shop manager only noticed his hands. He said that the little finger was missing from his left hand. The nails were well-kept but the forefinger of the right hand had a black rim.'

The smaller of Mary's bodyguards had arrived in the doorway, holding a bloodstained handkerchief to a badly-swollen nose.

'Stay where you are, Nigel,' Mary said, 'and try to keep out of trouble. Where's Eric?'

'How would I know?' Nigel retorted. The distortion of his voice produced by the broken nose, added to the effect of the hare-lip, made him almost unintelligible. 'Dangling himself in cold water, I should think. But we'll get even. You know what this bugger did—?'

'That'll do,' Mary said. Of the three others in the room, she exhibited the least hostility to Keith, but he had the feeling that this was because she was using her brain rather than her emotions.

'Eric wouldn't by any chance be fetching more armament from the car?' Keith enquired.

'We're not a guerilla group,' Mary said. 'The sum total of our armament is what you have in your hand.'

Mrs Winterton had examined the lighter without interest. 'I don't remember seeing it before,' she said.

Even from where he sat, Keith could see the initials. 'It has R.W. engraved on it,' he said.

'Those are very common initials,' the widow said.

Keith wondered just how far they would carry the charade. 'The police will be interested,' he said.

'I don't think that we should bother the police with something which is almost certainly irrelevant,' Mrs Winterton said.

'Oh, come on!' Keith said impatiently. 'Your husband was murdered and now this kind lady turns up with an obvious clue and a description of a man who may be the murderer. Of course you must tell the police.'

Mrs Winterton glared at him. 'You're the executor,'

she said. 'You tell them.'

'I will,' Keith said. 'Leave it on the table for the moment. I don't suppose there are any prints left on it, but there's no sense in adding any more. I'll take charge of it, and if it turns out not to be part of the estate, Mrs . . .' he had to think for a moment before her married name came to him '. . . Anguillas will get it back.'

'Too kind,' Mary Bruce said. 'And now, shouldn't you be running along?'

Keith had been about to ask what they had taken away from Steven Clune's bungalow but he changed his mind. Whatever it was, she did not have it with her. Nor did the two men. It might, of course, already be in the house, in which case he would have time to go after it later. More probably, it was in the car. He got out of his chair. Neither woman moved as he wrapped the lighter in his handkerchief – awkwardly, because he was still holding the revolver – and dropped it into one of the poacher's pockets in his olive-green shooting-coat.

At the door, he stopped and looked Nigel in the eye. 'If you follow me, I'll kill you,' he said and emphasised the words with a gesture with the pistol. He walked out into the hall. Eric was emerging from a door set between the drawing room and the front of the house. He seemed to be walking with care. He stopped dead when he saw Keith and leaned against the doorpost. Behind him, Keith saw a small cloakroom.

'I'm going,' Keith said. 'You stay out of sight or I'll shoot you where it hurts already!' He went out through the front door and closed it behind him.

Standing between the cars, he looked back. The windows of the drawing room were round the side of the house. Nobody was watching him. The Granada

91

was locked, doors and boot. Keith muttered something about suspicious sods. If the revolver had been a more trustworthy weapon, he would have been quite prepared to blow the boot-lock off. But that would have fetched them out and provoked another confrontation.

There were still no eyes at the front of the house, but he could feel Ronnie watching him.

Keith stooped and ran his fingers along the inside of the back bumper. It was only a one-in-three chance and he grinned to himself when it came off. His fingers found a small, magnetic box which came away in his hand. It contained a spare key. Mary had always had a fear of locking herself out of a car.

In the boot, he found a polythene bag containing what seemed to be a woman's brown leather or plastic handbag. The boot was otherwise empty.

He was still unobserved, except by Ronnie and Deborah, but it would not be long before those in the house wondered why they had not heard the sound of his jeep. He started its engine and then walked backwards across a few yards of grass to the ubiquitous rhododendrons, watching the windows as he went. When he was out of sight from the house, he turned at right angles away from the drive and hurried between the bushes for fifty yards before stopping to search for what he wanted. He found it, an old rabbit-hole half-filled with leaves and loose earth where he could bury the bag for the moment without leaving a trace for anybody who might follow him. In the deep shade, there was no undergrowth to retain the marks of his passing, just hard, bare earth. He looked around, to be sure that he could find the place again, and then hurried back to the cars, brushing mould from his fingers.

There was still nobody at the front of the house. He

shrugged and produced the revolver from where, after making sure that there was an empty chamber under the hammer, he had stowed it in his waistband. He paused to switch off the jeep's engine.

Once back inside the front door, he could hear the sound of argument from the drawing room. He would have liked to listen. But it would be better not to let them see earth on his fingers. And the lemonade was suddenly beginning to make its presence felt. He slipped through the first door. The cloakroom gave on to a small compartment with a wash-basin, which in turn led to what he most needed. . . .

It took him some time to wash the grit off his hands. The soap itself seemed to be gritty. When he emerged and walked softly to the still half-open door of the drawing room, the argument had stopped.

'I still haven't heard the bugger drive off,' said Eric's voice.

'Just be patient,' Mary said.

Keith peeped cautiously round the edge of the door but there were still no other guns in evidence. 'If you're waiting for me to go,' he said, coming into the room, 'you'll have to be very patient. I've decided that this is a good time to ask Mrs Winterton to show me over the house.'

He was blistered by the combined glare of four pairs of eyes.

'It will not be convenient,' Mrs Winterton said coldly.

Keith smiled. 'Yes, it will,' he said.

Mary Bruce sat back in her chair. 'We can wait until Mrs Winterton is free.'

'You'll have a long wait. I'm staying outside until morning.'

Mary Bruce froze for a second and then gave in gracefully. She got up. 'Very well,' she said.

Despite his broken nose, Nigel still had some spirit left. He took a pace towards Keith. 'Now look,' he said.

Keith aligned the barrel of the revolver on the middle of Nigel's forehead. 'You look,' he said.

'That's my shooter you took off Eric,' Nigel said plaintively. 'He'd no business parting with it. We're not going to shoot you and you're not going to shoot us. Let's have it back.'

'All right,' Keith said. He lowered his hand suddenly as if the heavy pistol was slipping out of his grasp. And as Nigel stooped, Keith seized his nose with his left hand and tweaked it firmly. As he backed away with the revolver still ready, Nigel was roaring with pain.

'Come along, boys,' Mary Bruce said, 'before the bastard thinks of anything worse to do to you.' Nose in the air, she led the way out. Her bodyguards followed, Nigel nursing his again bleeding snout. Eric, still walking like a cripple, detoured to pass well clear of Keith. He kept his eyes averted, perhaps, Keith thought sadly, to hide the hate in them.

Keith had intended to keep them too angry to think of looking in the Granada's boot and in this he was successful. He followed them as far as the front door. A short argument on the gravel was resolved by Mary taking the wheel. The two toughs stowed themselves gently in the back and the Granada set off, slowly and rather unsteadily, down the drive.

Keith was still holding the revolver. He broke it open, centred the empty chamber again under the hammer, snapped it shut and stowed it in the other poacher's pocket opposite the table-lighter. He found that the weight was dragging him to one side, but he preferred to have it with him, just in case.

The widow met him in the hall. She was regally gracious, as if there were no mystery, and she tried to gloss over the recent, angry scenes and the violence. 'I'm sure you mean well,' she said. 'But was it necessary to be so rough?' Keith could see a hundred signs of stretched nerves, from the quaver in her voice to the clasped hands.

'Now that they've gone,' he said gently, 'wouldn't you like to tell me something?'

'The place isn't as clean as I like it to be for visitors,' she said hurriedly (and indeed Keith could feel his feet gritting on the tiled floor), 'but on top of losing my maid, my daily woman has let me down. Refuses to work in a house where people get murdered, she says. I don't know what staff are coming to.'

Keith was tempted to mention that Molly had kept a similar house of almost the same size unaided for years. But Molly had grumbled for years and now had daily help.

'I'll make allowances,' he said. 'Is there a gardener?'

'A landscape contractor comes in once a fortnight.'

'Could I have the inventory,' Keith asked, 'just while we go round?'

'We'll start from the top,' the widow decided. She set off up the stairs before Keith could comment. 'I'm afraid my stepson has the inventory. Robin lent him some furniture and silver. I've asked him to mark on the inventory what he's keeping, so that you can deduct its value from his share of the estate.'

'Very thoughtful,' Keith said.

He made sure that he saw through the whole house,

attics and all. There were many places where pistols could have been hidden from him. But not two long Scottish muskets and the other longarms. He saw inside every cupboard and he looked behind and under the furniture. Mrs Winterton was still nervous, although she controlled it admirably, but she was no more nervous in one room than in another.

The house, although it had been very much a home, held a wealth of antiques which would have done credit to a small museum. Robin Winterton had obtained some treasures by inheritance and others by marriage, and he had not confined his investments entirely to guns. Keith, who had almost by the way picked up a knowledge of antiques during his pursuit of old firearms, saw that even without the gun collection the estate was far from valueless. A Minton vase in blue, cream and gold caught his eye. It bore the rare puce mark which had been used only on ceramics made for the 1862 Exhibition. There sat ten grand for a start, thought Keith.

Although it was bare, he made a point of looking in the cellar where the collection had been kept. She unset the alarms and unlocked a strongroom door to let him in. The old, stone barrel-vault was the same, but it hurt him almost physically to see the empty racks which had once held a well-chosen cross-section of the history of the gunmaker's art.

Two rooms, one on the first floor where Robin Winterton had met his fate and another at ground level where the killer had broken in, had been sealed by the police and Keith satisfied himself that the seals had not been tampered with. If anything had been hidden in those rooms before their arrival, the police would certainly have found it.

They had finished the tour and were returning to the hall when the telephone rang. The widow seated herself at a small table and picked up the instrument. Keith waited, partly out of unashamed curiosity.

'Yes,' Mrs Winterton said. 'You've only just heard from him? . . . Those seem to be the facts. . . . Yes, that's exactly what happened. . . . You can draw your own conclusions. . . . We'll speak again.' She hung up.

'Your stepson?' Keith asked.

'My son telephoned him about getting into a fight. I can't think why.'

Keith considered telling her that he now had the bag which had been taken from Steven Clune's bungalow, but it was against his instincts to give away information to somebody who was being far less than frank with him, or to play a card before he knew its exact value. He heard a vehicle in the drive and bade Mrs Winterton a curt farewell.

'I understood you to say that you would be staying,' she said.

'I'll be outside,' Keith said.

Ronnie's Land-Rover was grumbling up the drive. Keith met it at the corner of the house. Ronnie stopped and wound down his window.

'Well,' Keith said.

'We followed as far as Newbridge,' Ronnie said. 'When they got on the M-eight they speeded up and we lost them. They're going home, all right.'

'Maybe,' Keith said. 'If so, their whole ploy was a diversion to keep me busy around here while Danny does something slippery. On the other hand, they may have been leading you away in order to double back.'

'It didn't seem as if they knew we was there,' Ronnie

97

said doubtfully.

'They'd have to be pretty thick not to spot a Land-Rover in the mirror all this time,' Keith said. 'What do you think, Toots?'

Deborah considered and then gave judgment. 'Uncle Ronnie was clever,' she said, 'but I think they'd have known.'

'So do I,' Keith said. 'Well, we've got to back one horse or the other. I'm staying here overnight, Ronnie. I'm ninety per cent sure there's nothing in the house, but who could search these grounds? Leave Debbie with me; I'll get her another lift home. You go to Dunbar and keep an eye on Michael Winterton. I think he lives over the surgery and a vet would have a lot of storage space. Keep in touch with Molly.'

'That's all very well,' Ronnie said, 'but am I getting paid for all this running around?'

'If we've lost the guns,' Keith said, 'which is beginning to look more and more possible, I'll pay your fuel and that's your lot. But if we get them back. . . .'

'Aye? What, then?'

'Then I'll see you all right out of my profit for handling the guns. What are you after?'

'What I'd like,' Ronnie said dreamily, 'would be a really good rifle from one of the top makers, wi' a' the engraving gold-filled, just like that yin the Yank showed us last winter, an' wi' a real good telescopic sight and a night-sight to go wi' it.'

Keith shuddered. Ronnie was talking real money. On the other hand, Keith knew where he could pick up a suitably ornate rifle. If a top maker's name were added, Ronnie would never spot the difference. 'All right,' he said.

'You're on.'

SIX

The transmission-rumble, loose big-end and faulty exhaust of Ronnie's Land-Rover were still fading into the distance and Deborah was hardly into her customary myriad questions when a shining minibus with a multiplicity of aerials came up the drive. Recognising Philip Stratton's long face and silver hair behind the wheel, Keith waved it down.

'This is a cut above your old banger,' he commented.

Philip grinned at him. 'Like it? Office and sleeping-quarters when the news is breaking, ever since I turned freelance. Radio-telephone and the lot.'

'Would that include any food?'

'Some.'

'Open up, we're coming aboard. We've been forgetting to eat, lately.'

Philip parked in the shade where the Granada had stood. The Calders climbed into the back while he opened some tins and packets. The minibus had been planned and equipped with care. The miniature galley was adjoined by a desk complete with screwed-down typewriter and the telephone. There was a small black-and-white television. Opposite, a well-upholstered seat doubled as a single bunk.

'I don't really feel called on to feed you two guzzlers. I wouldn't bother,' Philip said, lighting the gas, 'except that I haven't had much eating-time myself.'

'I hoped that things were still slack.'

'They are. Pop-stars seem to have suffered an amazing onrush of chastity. Civil servants have been refusing bribes and keeping secrets. Even our politicians have been behaving with almost average common sense. The unions, for once, are allowing their members to earn some money. Aeroplanes are staying up and trains are staying down on the rails. All terribly, terribly boring. The economy, as usual, is stuck in the doldrums. But it's when there's no news that the journalist, and especially the freelance, has to rush around like a flea on a griddle if he's going to make ends meet. Here we are.' He put out three plates of tinned stew, complete with instant mashed potato and tinned spinach, and put the kettle on for coffee. 'One thing you learn, living this life, is to produce a meal at incredible speed. It's the one advantage you can gain over the others.'

'How would you like a story which combines missing artifacts of enormous value, fraud, two murders and the machinations of a celebrated fence?' Keith asked.

'Very much. But what artifacts? I heard that the late Mr Winterton had a collection of guns, which sounds like your scene.'

'You've got it,' Keith said, with his mouth full.

'Are they all that valuable?' Philip sounded disappointed.

'He had two original Scottish snaphaunce muskets,' Keith said impressively.

'So?'

Keith heaved a sigh. He was inclined to forget how ignorant others could be outside his immediate circle. 'You remember that pair of Scottish pistols which were auctioned a few years back?' he asked. 'They made the headlines.'

Philip might not know much about guns, but he remembered news. 'They made a hundred and sixty thousand, didn't they? Something like that? You don't mean that these will fetch that sort of price?'

'More,' Keith said. 'Much more. Guns tend to be worth more than other antiques. The thing you rest your bum on or put your clothes in, that could last for ever, but guns got out-of-date, were converted, adapted, broken, misused and eventually lost. On top of that, the original Scottish pistol's a great rarity. The English collected and destroyed every Scottish gun they could lay their hands on after the Bonnie Prince Charlie uprising. But, compared to pistols, the long gun's almost non-existent. You see, pistols were more easily hidden. Long guns are something else. Not one has ever come on the open market in Britain – nor anywhere else, as far as I know.'

Philip had abandoned his meal for a jotter and was scribbling hard. 'Tell me more,' he said. 'Weren't any more of them made later?'

'By the time it would've been permitted, the peak of workmanship had passed, fashions had changed and the new French lock had come in. The result was a new and less peculiarly Scottish style. The old one was very distinctive – a snaphaunce lock with sliding flashpan-cover, stock not shaped like the traditional gun but a single curve with a semi-circular bite out of it for the thumb, ball trigger and profuse decoration. You could

101

be forgiven for mistaking it for something Arab or oriental.'

Philip resumed his meal. 'All right, you've made your point. Tell me the tale,' he said.

'I'm going to,' Keith said. 'But, until we've settled a few details, I'm telling you in confidence. Under absolute embargo. Agreed?'

Philip nodded uncertainly.

'And I've got to squeeze my way between libel and slander,' Keith went on, 'so Deborah's here to bear witness that I haven't said a word. Nearly all of it's verifiable from other sources.

'On Monday night, Mrs Winterton called the police, who found that her husband had been battered to death by an intruder.

'Old Robin Winterton had been a canny chap. Instead of taking out an endowment policy, he had put all of his savings into antiques, mostly antique guns, starting from a few guns which had come to him through his first wife. Those had included the two Scottish long guns. And so he left a will, naming me as his executor. His assets were to be sold and he left substantial sums to his son and daughter by his first wife and the balance to his widow.

'On Thursday I came back from a trip and heard about the murder for the first time. There was a discussion in the office of Mr Enterkin, the solicitor in Newton Lauder, in which the widow blandly remarked that we didn't have to worry about the guns any more; she'd sold them to a dealer who'd knocked on the door the previous day, for two hundred quid. She hadn't even got his name.'

Philip was scribbling again. 'That's hard to believe,' he said. He stopped and looked hard at Keith. 'Did you

102

believe it?'

'Never mind my thoughts,' Keith said. 'I'm giving you checkable facts. I didn't know what to think. First thing next morning – yesterday – I dashed into Edinburgh. From Mrs Winterton's description, the man had sounded Edinburgh. Anyway, it was the obvious place to start.

'Mrs Winterton's description of the man and his van led me to Duncan Laurie's store in Waterman's Lane. I found him with his throat cut, apparently a suicide, but I've no doubt that by now the police are treating it as murder. They probably intend to issue a statement on Monday morning. Mrs Winterton had said that he stowed some of the guns in a dower chest, and there was just such a chest in his store.'

'Why are you so sure that he was murdered?' Philip asked.

Even in confidence, Keith was not going to admit that he had risked disturbing a murder scene. The police were inclined to get uptight about such things, and his business depended on maintaining at least superficially good relations with the force. 'I'm not prepared to give my reasons at the moment,' he said. 'They're irrelevant. The police will have their own reasons by now.'

'I can check.'

'Go ahead.'

'Later,' Philip said. 'Finish the story.'

'This morning, Mary Anguillas turned up on my doorstep. She used to be Mary Bruce. Danny Bruce's daughter,' Keith added when Philip still looked blank. 'She had a couple of toughs with her in the car, a fawn Granada.'

Philip sat up suddenly. 'Danny Bruce of Glasgow? I

103

remember now. You had a run-in with him, years ago. Your evidence sent him away. Under cover of a couple of genuine antique shops, he'd been operating as a fence in a very big way of business. The daughter kept the shops running until he came out.'

'That's Mary for you,' Keith said. 'All heart and very much her daddy's girl. And I still don't know whether Danny had got wind that the guns were adrift and sent her to find out or if the whole thing was a diversion, to keep me running around in circles here while Danny stowed the guns away or got them out of the country. Part of the time, she seemed to be fishing to find out how much I'd offer to get them back.

'I passed my wife a note to phone her brother to follow them when they left. And again, I still don't know whether they knew they were being followed and either didn't care or wanted it that way.

'I wanted to know a bit more about the family. Steven Clune, the widow's son by her first marriage, was the only one I hadn't met, so I drove there. And I damn near caught up with Mary Bruce again. She and her boys left, taking something away with them. And when I went inside, I found Steven Clune with his hands still tied, badly beaten up, terrified, very much upset but determined not to tell me anything.

'When I phoned my wife, I got a message to say that my brother-in-law was still on their tail and that they seemed to be heading here. So I followed along, and here they were sure enough, closeted with the widow. One of them pulled this on me.' With some relief, Keith pulled out the revolver, which had been both unbalancing and digging into him, and laid it on the desk.

'Hey! I didn't know about that,' Deborah said. 'Can I

104

have it for my collection when this is over?'

'Certainly not,' Keith said. 'The police will probably need it. Anyway, you wouldn't want it. It's only a cheap, Belgian copy. Nasty, dangerous thing.'

Philip refused to be diverted. 'Go on,' he said.

'That's about it. I made it clear that I could stick around longer than they could and, after they left, my brother-in-law saw them well on the road to Glasgow. But, just in case they doubled back, I've sent him over to keep an eye on Michael Winterton's place at Dunbar and I'm going to stick around here. While I was ministering to Steven Clune, Deborah got a good look through his place and we're pretty sure that the guns aren't there.

'One other thing. I was careful to keep the visitors too angry to think of looking in their boot before they left. Because I'd got it open and lifted what they took from Steven Clune. I've got it buried not far from here, and that's where it stays until I can deliver it to the cops. The only way I can see it is that Danny Bruce had got wind of something over one of his several grape-vines and needed it in order to put pressure on the family. But, as far as I can make out through a polythene bag, it's a perfectly ordinary woman's handbag. And how that can be blackmail material I can't for the moment think.'

'Especially with Steven Clune being the way he is,' Deborah put in mischievously.

'Well, I can,' Philip said. A stir of excitement took over from the professional detachment in the reporter's voice. 'This could be serious. Let's take a look at it.'

'Let's not,' Keith said. 'I'm not doing any more tampering with evidence. I may leave it lying until I'm sure I've finished with it, but if I go on digging it up and

105

putting it back I'm going to lead somebody else to it sooner or later. It's your turn. Cough up.'

Philip shrugged. 'There's one handbag the police have been looking for for months.' He glanced sideways at Deborah and then back to Keith. 'You remember the Jean Watson case in Granton?'

'No,' Keith said. His attention to the news was highly selective. He rarely watched television and only skimmed the papers, occasionally catching up with the news via his car radio.

'Well, I do,' Deborah said. 'Rape and murder,' she added with relish.

'That's right,' Philip said. 'But if you won't dig it up, we can only guess.'

'Then we're guessing,' Keith said. 'For the moment, exactly what it is doesn't matter. The fact that Danny Bruce wanted a hold over the family suggests that the guns are still around here.'

'You don't know that,' Philip said. 'If Danny Bruce organised the whole thing, he may only have wanted to squeeze a – what do you call it? – a provenance out of the family, the documentation which would make it easier for him to sell the collection.'

'I wish you hadn't said that,' Keith said after a pause. 'It complicates things still further. Yet it's just another argument for what I was going to do anyway. And this is where you come in.'

'I thought it might be,' Philip said. 'Can I have this, exclusive?'

'No, you can't,' Keith snapped. 'I called on you for help, not to make you a gift of it. Mostly, do you write up the whole story yourself and sell it as a package?'

'Usually.'

'Do you ever tip off all the papers to a story?'

'If it's impossible for me to handle alone,' Philip said. 'Then, I'll tip off the papers and they give me a fee for the tip.'

'That's what I thought,' Keith said. 'What I want most just now is for a whole army to start watching this place and Michael Winterton's home and Danny Bruce and anybody and everything relevant. I want them poking everywhere so that, wherever the guns are, nobody can move them. Then I can do some more chasing for myself. Otherwise, I'm stuck here, just in case. And where else can I find an army of nosy beggars at a weekend except reporters?'

Philip Stratton scratched his head and took a long drink of coffee. 'You could be right,' he said. 'But you're sure you want me to tell them the value of the guns? They might find them. And they're not all as far beyond temptation as I am.'

'They couldn't sell them. I could, Danny Bruce probably could, they certainly couldn't. Not without being caught,' Keith said. 'I know every dealer and major collector in the Western Hemisphere. I know which ones could be approached with a dodgy deal without word leaking out. Anybody outside the trade trying to hock anything so rare would find himself the centre of a glare of publicity, with the police and myself on his back, within half a day. Make sure they understand that.'

Philip put his mug down with a bang. 'All right,' he said. 'If the police confirm that Duncan Laurie was murdered, I'll go ahead. But you'll have to promise a press conference and a statement in the not too distant future.'

'Fair enough,' Keith said. 'Let's make it Monday afternoon.'

'Tomorrow evening,' Philip said firmly. 'They won't wait any longer. And I get your personal story, exclusive, when it's over.'

The police are in the business of gathering information rather than divulging it, and Saturday evening is not the best time for tracking down the man who knows the answer and is both prepared and empowered to release it, but in the end Philip obtained confirmation that the death of Duncan Laurie was being treated as murder.

'Fair enough,' he said to Keith. 'Give me time to make a few calls and there'll be a dozen reporters and photographers on the job by morning – provided that nothing else breaks in the meantime. If the Russians make angry noises or the wrong person lands pregnant, you'll be lucky to see one copy-boy being given his chance as a cub reporter. That's the way it goes. I can keep you company overnight if you want.'

'Better not,' Keith said. 'I'd rather you ran the lassie back to her mother. Any messages will be coming to my home, and Molly's got no way to get them to me. You can bring me the word in the morning.'

'You're not pulling any kind of a fast one on me?'

'Just holding the fort. If anything happens during the night, you'll hear all about it.'

'See that I do.'

The minibus cruised gently away down the drive. Philip, no doubt, would be questioning Deborah all the way to Newton Lauder, but as far as Keith could remember she knew nothing which he would prefer to keep from the press.

Shadows were lengthening. One or two lights came on in the house; otherwise, there was no sign of the widow.

Keith circled the house, keeping well back in the undergrowth. There was no sign of disturbed ground. He found a summerhouse, a detached garage and a toolshed, but none of them contained anything of more interest than a Mercedes drophead. Soon it was too dark to search further.

He made his way back and approached the drive obliquely. After a little exploration, he settled himself between two rhododendrons. The place, where it was not walled, was well fenced and a visitor, on foot or with a vehicle, would pass within a few yards of him.

He waited, with the patience of the experienced stalker. Only the stars were out. The night was warm, he was not uncomfortable and the noises of the night, which would have unsettled any town-bred watcher, were as familiar to him as the ticking of his study clock. An owl was hunting nearby.

He must have slept, but that did not matter; he knew that any change in the pattern of sound would have awakened him. A brilliant moon was up and the night was quiet with the silence which precedes the dawn, but he knew that something had roused him. A sound, half-heard, came back into his memory. A car had stopped out in the road.

Keith smiled grimly in his dark bower. He had the revolver and his knife; and he would have the advantage of surprise.

Something rustled, not far away, and it was not one of the small animals which had been around him earlier. He made ready for a shadow which would pass between himself and the moonlit grass. A twig snapped, further away this time. How many were coming? It had gone quiet again.

The car at the road started up and drove away.

Keith waited, ten minutes, twenty, half an hour, but there was no more movement. Nobody had passed him, he could swear. He moved softly to one side, to a position near where he had sat with Ronnie and Deborah to study the front of the house. And there he saw the answer, the black silhouette of his jeep against the moonlight beyond. Somebody had come to see if he was as good as his word and, seeing his jeep and knowing that Keith would not be far away, had departed.

He shrugged, sat down and allowed himself to dose again. There was nothing to be gained by kicking himself. He would rather have kicked Mary Bruce, or that damned moon.

The minibus was back before the sun was high and reversed in beside the jeep again. This time Philip Stratton was alone, and Keith, as he climbed inside, felt a sense almost of bereavement. He had become used to the sometimes irritating but always interesting presence at his side.

'The *Scotsman* and the *Glasgow Herald* will have men out within the next hour or so. The others will take longer. Your wife sends greetings,' Philip said, 'and also this and this,' passing over a clean shirt, a disposable razor and a sealed envelope, 'also some breakfast which I will now proceed to fry for us both.'

Molly's note, in her round and somehow very suitable hand, ran:

> Ronnie phoned. Nothing happening at Dunbar. Will phone again later.
>
> Two different lots of police phoned. Chief Inspector Ovenstone from Edinburgh wants

another statement from you. No hurry, whenever suits you. (A phone-number followed.)

And Inspector Cathcart, Strathclyde, phoned. Wants you to know that Danny Bruce had some heavy boxes moved into an outbuilding behind Golightly's Music Shop in Falkirk. If there's any chance of nailing D.B. again, or his daughter, he'll come running.

Try to be good. M.

Keith passed the note to Philip, who scanned it quickly. 'Could you call Molly for me?' Keith asked. 'Tell her, when Ronnie calls, to ask him to look into this Falkirk thing.'

'Now?'

'After you've made my breakfast,' Keith said. First things always came first. 'I'm surprised Edinburgh doesn't sound more urgent.'

'What else could you tell them?'

'Nothing. But they don't know that.'

A car bearing a PRESS sticker – the first of many, Keith hoped – came bustling up the drive as Keith, refreshed and tidy, prepared to depart. He squeezed past and drove away. Philip would brief the arrivals and Keith had already made up his mind that he would only answer questions from the police, and not too many of those.

But it was to the police that Keith went first.

There is no respite in murder enquiries. On the other hand, every policeman must have some time off in the week and Sunday overtime is expensive. The nearest police station was manned only by a clerkess who directed him to a mobile headquarters parked behind

111

the building. Here he found the team investigating Robin Winterton's murder, represented at the moment by a plain-clothes detective inspector and a uniformed w.p.c. Other desks were unmanned and the end wall was screened by a curtain.

The two officers were indulging in a little flirtatious badinage when Keith interrupted them. The inspector, who had compensated for this compromising intrusion by standing on his dignity at first, thawed when Keith introduced himself as the executor of the estate.

'Not that we can do much more out here,' Inspector Fleet said, over a cup of tea brewed by the w.p.c. 'In fact, we could unseal those rooms if the old lady's being inconvenienced. We've done all the searches and enquiries around here that you could think of. From now until something breaks, the real work goes on in Edinburgh and in liaison with other forces. Sooner or later, somebody'll talk too loud in a pub, or try to sell something from the house, or get lifted for something else and cough this one. Then it'll all start again. Until then, it's wait and pray.'

'I may have what you're waiting and praying for,' Keith said. He produced the table-lighter. 'I was at Halleydane House late yesterday, and a lady from Bruce, the antique dealers in Buchanan Street, Glasgow, arrived with this. Mrs Winterton agrees that her husband had one like it, but she wouldn't identify it despite the initials. I'm afraid it's been handled by the world and his wife. It was sold to them by a youngish man with a finger missing off his left hand. The shop manager was quoted as saying that his hands were well kept except for a black-rimmed first finger on the right hand. To me, that suggests a pipe-smoker.'

The inspector allowed himself to look faintly

112

pleased. 'I'll go and see the old lady myself,' he said.

Keith was on the point of warning the inspector that the place might be hopping with reporters, but decided that that would only provoke questions which he was not yet ready to answer. 'I hope you can pin her down,' he said. 'I couldn't.'

'Strathclyde can visit the dealer tomorrow. With a description like that ...' The inspector stopped. 'Bruce? That wouldn't be *Danny* Bruce?'

'I believe so,' Keith said. 'The fence.'

'You know that, do you?' Inspector Fleet frowned and tapped an irregular rhythm on the desk. 'Why would Danny Bruce be sending a lady all this way on the chance that something he'd bought was stolen? His usual form would be to rub his hands and use it to pressure the seller into doing a few more little jobs for him.'

'I wondered the same thing myself,' Keith said. 'It may be that he thinks that withholding evidence in a murder case is too hot even for him.'

'Since when did Danny Bruce think that way?' the inspector asked rhetorically. 'The story doesn't stand up, but the description sounds circumstantial enough to be real.'

As he drove off, Keith was more concerned over a different question. The police were treating Duncan Laurie's death as murder. They would have found Danny Bruce's name in Laurie's diary. Keith had pointed out a possible link between the two deaths. So why had the inspector not jumped out of his chair when Danny Bruce's name cropped up again?

The brown handbag, still in its polythene cover, was in the back of the jeep. Keith had come with the intention of handing it over. But if Inspector Fleet was being kept in the dark by his colleagues, why should Keith enlighten him about something quite unconnected with his own case?

The wallpaper above Mrs Winterton's telephone had been pristine, unblemished by the scrawled phonenumbers with which less house-proud folk desecrate their walls. The telephone sat on a glass-topped table, and beneath the glass Keith had noticed a single business-card, presumably that of the business most frequently telephoned. It was the card of a local taxi firm and he had noted the address.

The firm proved to be a small one, run from a modest house in a large village and conveniently close to the local garage. One low-priced but well-kept saloon stood at the door, its roof carrying an illuminable sign with the name Moir and a phone-number.

A stout woman with a cheerful face answered the door to Keith's ring, drying her hands on an apron. 'Were you wanting a taxi?' she asked. 'My husband's away with the other one, but I could take you as long as it isn't for more than an hour. The kirk-goers,' she added in explanation. She reached for a chauffeur's cap and popped it on to a head covered with ginger curls, an incongruous and deliberately comic picture.

'I don't need a taxi,' Keith said, smiling. 'I'm Mr Winterton's executor and I was wondering whether there are any outstanding accounts.'

'You'd better come inside,' Mrs Moir said. She took him into what Keith could only think of as a living-kitchen and offered him an old but comfortable wing-chair. She began to riffle through an untidy pile of paper on a sideboard. 'I think they were up-to-date,' she said. 'Mr Winterton – poor old chap – was a prompt payer and the old lady always paid cash. Took a pride in it. Liked to let you see that she was carrying a big bundle of notes. She was the one I'd have expected to be mugged, carrying all that money around. I warned her more than once. No, there's nothing outstanding.'

'They used you a lot, did they?' Keith asked.

She went back to her washing-up, bouncing her voice back to him off the wall above the sink. 'He didn't, not unless he was going by train or plane. She used us whenever she went anywhere without him. She said her husband reckoned it was cheaper than running a second car. Maybe so, but my guess is that he didn't want her to drive. He wasn't daft; she's not the type to give way to anybody, whether it's her right of way or not.'

Keith suppressed a chuckle. She had summed up his own view of the widow to a nicety. 'Do you know whether your husband took her to Edinburgh on Monday?'

'He didn't. He was away to Gorebridge to fetch a mannie whose car had broken down. I took her myself in the other car. Dropped her right outside the Queen's Theatre, where her friends were already waiting for her.'

'And fetched her back?'

'No. One of her friends would have taken her home. That was the usual arrangement. Happened about every second week.'

'I see . . . .' Keith said slowly. 'And when you picked her up – do you mind my asking? – did you see Mr Winterton?'

She glanced at him over her shoulder. 'Bless you, I don't mind,' she said. 'The police already asked the same things and you've a right to know, you being his executor and all. I didn't see him but I heard her call

115

good night to him.'

'What else did the police ask you?'

'Nothing much. Only about times.'

'You've been very helpful,' Keith said. 'One more thing. I understand that Mrs Winterton had a resident maid until recently. Could you help me to find her? Were you, by any chance, called to take her to the bus station or somewhere?'

She turned round, laughing. 'I've known Bessie Dalry for years,' she said. 'Her family has a small farm just a few miles off. There's three other unmarried daughters, so Bessie takes domestic jobs from time to time. She's going to one of the big hotels, but she thought she'd have a week or two helping with the harvest first. I could take you there.'

'I have my own car,' Keith said.

'No harm offering. I'll draw you a map, then.'

Keith found the farm without difficulty. It stood on a clay soil but with, he judged, a good tilth and a slope to the south. The buildings were compact but solid and well kept. As usual with a busy farm, it seemed at first glance to be deserted, but machines were crawling in the fields and he could hear somebody whistling among the outbuildings.

A stone wall enclosed an attractive garden in full flower at the front of the house, but he guessed that the front door was seldom used by visitors. He tucked the jeep out of sight – it was not a very impressive vehicle for making calls, stained as it was with bird-dung in white and purple – and found a back door standing open. The smell of baking made his mouth water. He rapped with his knuckles and a woman came to the door.

116

She was in her early thirties, slim and with an attractive air of fragility which he realised was probably deceptive – he had known women who looked just as feminine and frail but who could carry bags of corn or creels of peat long after the men around them were exhausted. She was not beautiful but her skin was good, her dark hair was lustrous and well-styled and her large, brown eyes, by far her best feature, looked ready to speak – to flash or twinkle – and Keith could imagine them languorous with love. The overall impression was alluring, but in a way which was wholesome rather than sensual.

'Who did you want?' she asked. 'The others are out in the fields. It may be the Lord's Day, but the harvest has to be got in when you've got the weather. If you spend the Sabbath in the kirk and it rains on the Monday, the barley gets spoiled just the same. I can't believe He'd want that.'

'I'm looking for Bessie Dalry,' Keith said.

'That's me.' She seemed surprised that anyone would want her.

Keith introduced himself. 'I'm Mr Winterton's executor,' he finished.

Her face clouded. She went back to making sandwiches, but her movements were slow and mechanical. 'That was a terrible thing,' she said. 'I was so sad when I heard. He was a fine man, and he deserved better than he got. Sit you down. But you needn't bother to tell me that he left me nothing, because he told me that before I left.'

Keith took a Windsor chair. 'Can I help?' he asked

She brightened again. 'Thanks but no. It's just the men's dinner-pieces and they're about finished. Take one if you'd like.'

117

'Why did he tell you a thing like that?' Keith asked. 'It seems an odd thing to mention.' He took a sandwich and bit into it. Cold beef with a trace of mustard and pickle and a leaf of lettuce, in fresh bread which had never been inside a baker's shop.

His question seemed to flummox her. She turned away and poured water from a large kettle into an equally large teapot. 'He just did,' she said.

Keith could only think of one reason for her discomfiture. 'He gave you a present instead?'

She turned back towards him but shook her head without looking up, busying herself with stacking sandwiches into a plastic box.

'I'm his executor,' Keith said. 'I'll be seeing his cheques and I need to know about any gifts of cash.'

There was a brisk whirring outside and a Citröen 2cv dashed up to the door. A younger woman, but so like Bessie that she had to be a sister, came in. She nodded incuriously to Keith. 'They'll be looking for their dinner in a minute,' she said.

'It's ready.'

When the sandwiches and tea and some tins of beer were loaded into the back of the Citröen, the little car bustled away again. A plate of sandwiches remained on the scrubbed table. 'You have those,' Bessie said. 'I'll make myself an egg.' She poured more water into a smaller teapot.

'Thanks,' Keith said. He waited until she met his eye. 'How much did he give you?'

'Five hundred pounds,' she said, blushing. 'I didn't want to say, because I'd heard that a gift made just before somebody died could be taken back. Partly that.'

'I don't think you need to worry about it. And it was

118

partly the amount that worried you, wasn't it? Five hundred pounds is more than you'd give to a maid who'd been nothing else. I won't tell anybody,' Keith added.

She walked to the door, looked out and then returned. When she spoke, it was very softly. 'He wanted to make it more, but that was as much as I'd let him give me.' Her blush was subsiding. 'I'd been there for eleven years, almost since I left school.'

'And you were lovers?'

'That's just a word,' she said.

'You were his mistress, then?'

She half-laughed. 'I couldn't say that I was ever that. But he was a grand man and yet I was sorry for him. He had his needs, the same as any other man, and she wasn't for any of that sort of thing. She'd married him for position and for company, though she was aye grumbling that she didn't get enough of either. He'd no sort of life of it at all. So he turned to me.'

'Did his wife know?'

'I'm sure of it,' she said, 'but she never seemed to care. They slept apart anyway. After the first few years he was getting old, too old to master me the way a man should. But he still liked a cuddle, and there's things a woman can still do for an old man, if she's fond of him.' She touched her eyes with a handkerchief. 'What must you think of me?'

'I hope there's somebody like you around when I grow old,' Keith said gently. 'Why did you leave, then?'

'I was sorry to be parted from him,' she said frankly, 'and the work wasn't hard, but it got that I couldn't thole her at any price. And the rows inside that family, even with both sons away from home, you'd scarcely believe! But you surely don't want to be hearing all this

119

talk, and about a mannie that's not long dead.'

'That's what I came to you for,' Keith said. 'There've been some funny goings-on with the valuables and I need to know all I can find out. It seemed to me that you'd be the best person to tell me.'

She sat down opposite him with her boiled egg and buttered a slice of that bread. Keith was surprised to realise that he had eaten all the sandwiches. There was a large, terracotta mug of tea in front of him.

'If I don't get away from here soon,' she said, 'I'll be getting fat.'

'You're the thin type,' Keith said. 'You'll never get fat. Anyway . . . is this your own baking?'

'Yes.'

'It would be a self-inflicted wound then. Just tell me about the family, whatever comes into your mind.'

She finished her small meal, pushed her plate away and lit a cigarette. 'When I first went there,' she said, 'they were already married and settled in and their two sons were away from home, neither of them married but living their separate lives. His daughter, Miss Gwen, was still at home then, although she married soon after and went off to Canada. Mr Winterton was not long retired, I think.

'It wasn't so bad then, though I think he was already seeing that he'd made a sair mistake. The mistress had – has – the devil's own temper. She never lost the heid, mind, it might've been better if she had. But she was thrawn. If he didn't give in to her at every turn, there'd be a silence so cold you could feel it right through the house.

'The one thing she could never make him do was to give up his guns. He tried to explain that they were an investment, but she'd not listen. I think she was jealous

120

of them, not of me. But he'd not give in to her on that. The guns were all he'd got.'

'And you,' Keith said.

'Maybe. The real stramash started when she found out about her own son, Mr Clune. You ken about him?'

'Yes. Poor sod,' Keith said.

'Aye. Until then, he'd been his mother's boy. Not being a driver, she'd never been to where he lived. But one day she took Mr Moir's taxi and went to see that he was being looked after. What she saw she didn't like one bit. She came back to Halleydane House in such a taking you'd think it was the end of the world coming. Her husband tried to explain such things to her – I think he'd guessed what was up with the boy some time before – but she'd not listen, and when he said that she'd made the boy turn that way she went into a sulk that lasted a fortnight. After that, it was as if her own son had never existed and instead she was all over her stepson, Mr Michael.

'But Mr Winterton was scunnered wi' his own son, who was aye after him for money, being on the wild side and a devil with drink and women and betting and the like. He took the part of Mr Clune, being sorry for him.

'So there they were, split in two camps, her with his son and him with hers. Any time there was a stishie, that's how they'd take sides. And she'd aye be expecting him to dance attendance, but when he did she'd be that off-hand with him he'd go off and sit with his guns.

'That's what drove me out of the house in the end. She never stopped yattering at him to leave his guns alone. He was to sell them off and be a proper husband to her – not that she'd let him be that. It got so bad that

121

I couldn't bide there any longer. I cried when I said goodbye to him.'

'I could cry now,' Keith said. 'I liked the old chap. He never let on that he was unhappy. God, what a way to end his days!'

Before leaving the farm, Keith borrowed the telephone and called his wife. Molly, it seemed, had been waiting anxiously for his call.

'Mr Donelly was on the phone at lunch-time,' she said.

It took Keith a few seconds to pin down the name. Then it came back to him. 'The french polisher and repairer?'

'That's the one,' Molly said.

'What did he have to say?'

'Not a lot. He seemed concerned about ten quid he said you promised he could have, to split with some barmaid. I believed him, because it sounded exactly like you. He gave me his address. And I found out that he works with Dougall and Symington. That's a small cabinetmaker's firm at Craiglockhart. He was phoning from there. Apparently, they've got an urgent job on.'

Keith conjured up his mental map and looked at his watch. 'That's this side of Edinburgh,' he said. 'I've just got time to look him up. Any news from Ronnie?'

'Nothing. But, Keith, Mr Enterkin came out specially to say that before his secretary gave Mrs Winterton the inventory she took a photocopy of it. It's here now. Do you want it?'

'Do I!' Keith said. 'I want it like blazes. But I don't have time to come home just yet. I've got to give a press conference at Halleydane House in a couple of hours.'

'Do you? What fun!'

'If you think that,' Keith said, 'you can give it.'

'I would if I knew what to say. What are you going to say, Keith?'

'Damned if I know. It depends what I can find out between now and then. Could you hop into the car and bring it to me at Halleydane House?'

'Yes, of course. I'd love to.' Molly had been wondering what excuse she could make to attend the press conference. 'I'll put on a funny hat and my glasses and make out I'm representing *Woman's Realm*. How do I get there?'

'Bring Deborah. She should know the way by now.'

The firm of Dougall and Symington, being the sort of business mainly patronised by collectors and by those in the trade, was not easy to find. Keith, after the usual experience of discovering that the passers-by were all foreigners with cleft palates, happened upon that great rarity, a local resident who not only knew the whereabouts of his destination but was able to give directions which turned out to be accurate. He parked the jeep in a shaded yard where several small businesses existed and even seemed to thrive. The others were shuttered in Sabbath calm, but the double doors marked by a small plate with the firm's name stood ajar. Keith knocked and entered.

It was a general-purpose workshop about the size of two squash-courts, smelling pleasantly of glue and varnish, hardwoods and warm machinery. Two men were at work. The nearer, a small man with a simian face, straightened his back and came to meet him, scowling.

'Is Mike Donelly here?' Keith asked.

123

'That's myself.' The voice was faintly Glasgow-Irish.

'I'm Keith Calder. You phoned my home. I wanted to ask you—'

'About Duncan Laurie. I bet you did. But first. . . .'

Keith produced a ten pound note. It seemed to vanish before it was quite out of his wallet. Donelly still did not smile, but at least he was scowling less. 'I can't spare long,' he said. 'This is wanted by mid-week. What did you want to know?'

'You used to give Laurie a hand in the evenings?' Keith asked.

'Most evenings. Just to clean up or mend whatever he'd bought.'

'Did he ever say anything about a collection of antique guns?'

Donelly looked blank. 'Not a word.'

'Do you know where he was working earlier in the week, up to the time he died?'

'Let's see, now. Monday and Tuesday, he was on the knock between here, Peebles and Galashiels. He didn't go far – that old van of his was on the blink and if it was going to let him down he'd rather it was near home.'

'And Wednesday?' Keith asked.

'About Wednesday I can't tell you, not of my own certain knowledge,' Donelly said carefully. 'Wednesday evening I had to visit my sister in hospital, and that's when he was killed, d'you see? Leastways, the police are now saying he was killed. They called it suicide at first. If I'd gone to meet Duncan as usual, he'd've said where he'd been.'

'If he was still alive.'

'That's right. Maybe I'd have saved him. Or maybe I'd have been done as well.'

'But did he tell you, on Tuesday, where he was going

to go the next day?' Keith persisted.

'He did that. But whether he did as he said he would or not. . . .' Donelly paused hopefully.

Keith produced another fiver. 'This is the last,' he said.

'The garage was taking the van in for the day. Duncan thought he'd take the train to Glasgow. There were one or two small pieces the Edinburgh dealers wouldn't give him his price for, so he thought he'd try through in the west. And he was to deliver an ormolu clock one of the dealers had bought over the phone for a special customer.'

'Danny Bruce?' Keith said.

'I believe that was the name. It was Rutherglen Gardens, if that helps. It was a cash deal, not to go through the books, so Duncan was to take it to the dealer's home.'

'Gardens?' Keith said. 'Bloody Gardens?'

'That's right.'

Keith was staring vacantly at the ceiling while he digested this fresh information and he was only vaguely aware of the phone ringing and of the voice of the other craftsman. 'Are you Mr Calder?'

'He is,' Donelly said.

'If you can wake him up, tell him he's wanted on the phone.'

Keith came out of his reverie and crossed the workshop to take the phone. It was Philip Stratton. Distortion of his voice suggested that he was using his radio-telephone. 'Is that you, Keith?'

'Yes.'

'Thank God for that! Molly phoned me. She was just about to leave to come here when she got a call from the police in Falkirk to say that they had you in custody. She was sure that you couldn't have reached Craiglockhart yet, let alone Falkirk if you'd changed your mind and headed that way. But no woman ever had a sense of time, so I couldn't be sure. Can you make sense of it?'

'Oh yes,' Keith said. 'No trouble at all. Is Molly on her way?'

'Yes. That's why she asked me to call you.'

'I'm coming back right away, or even sooner,' Keith said. 'Look after Molly when she arrives – I think something's going to happen. And see if you can contact the detective inspector who's on duty in the mobile HQ. His name was Fleet, I think. Or possibly Feet. Tell him that if he cares to meet me at Halleydane House, I should have something useful for him.'

He hung up. Deep in thought, he stared at the box in front of him and only realised slowly what he was seeing. 'Is this the urgent job you're working on?' he asked.

'That's it,' said Donelly. 'I'm putting on an antique finish while Jim makes the brasswork. It's a rough old job, but the customer's in a hell of a hurry.'

'Do you know who it's for?'

'Not the faintest idea,' Donelly said cheerfully. 'Cash customer. He paid half in advance and he's coming in for it on Wednesday.'

'Good God!' Keith said. 'It all fits together.'

'I'd bloody well hope so,' Donelly said. 'The customer would soon complain if it didn't.'

SEVEN

Keith tore the jeep out of Edinburgh past the massed cars of Sunday golfers at Fairmilehead and swung off on to the Peebles road.

As he went, he wondered what inspiration had led Ronnie to identify himself to the arresting officers as Keith Calder. Could his brother-in-law have suffered a sudden onrush of intelligence? But he remembered that Ronnie had, during their wilder past, often used his name when confronted by hostile officers and he had occasionally returned the dubious compliment. Old habits, it seemed, died hard.

As he drove, part of his mind shuffled the known facts. The remainder was willing the miles away.

The gravel sweep at Halleydane House would be choked with reporters' cars. Rather than add to the congestion, Keith turned through the gates and then swung hard off the drive through a narrow gap in the undergrowth. Leaving the jeep, he hurried across the lawn towards the house.

A car overtook him on the drive, only a few yards away but out of his sight. If this were Danny Bruce or any permutation of his relatives and retainers, he would be swallowed whole by the reporters. But surely he would have telephoned and been told that the house was under siege?

Looking ahead, Keith saw that all was not as expected. Instead of a huddle of press cars, Philip Stratton's minibus and his own hatchback stood opposite the front door. Two men were getting out of a police-car at the corner of the house, and that was all.

Keith broke into a run. Philip Stratton walked to meet him. As they met, Inspector Fleet came up with another man. A third policeman, the driver, waited in the car. 'Detective Chief Inspector Ovenstone was with me when your message came in,' Fleet said. 'He's in charge of the Duncan Laurie case. So I brought him along.'

'How d'you do,' Keith said. 'Philip—'

'So what's this new information?' Ovenstone asked. He was a large man, older than Fleet, with a bald head but hair sprouting elsewhere like weeds through broken paving. His nostrils and ears were particularly well provided.

'Hang on a moment, please. Philip. What happened? I was expecting reporters by the dozen. Wouldn't they come?'

'They came,' Philip said. 'The place had been buzzing all day. But—'

'I want to know what this is about,' Ovenstone said loudly.

'And so you shall,' Keith said. 'Just as soon as we all hear what's happened. Philip . . .'

'About ten minutes ago,' Philip said, 'a taxi arrived at the door. A man driving, no passenger.'

'Moir?'

128

'That's right. Immediately, Mrs Winterton appeared on the steps. She said that if Mr So-and-so of the *Bootle Advertiser* was there – or something like that, I don't remember which paper she mentioned – there was a message for him. A helicopter had crashed in flames on top of the Lammermuirs with Prince Philip aboard and another member of the royal family and he was to get over there immediately with his photographer. Then she hopped into the taxi and went off.'

'What a load of horse-crap!' Keith said.

'That's what I thought and I said so. But none of them dared risk ignoring what might have turned out to be the story of the year. I tried to point out that if you've seen one incinerated royal you've seen the lot—'

'I'm surprised you stayed here yourself.'

'If there really was a chopper down,' Philip said, 'which I doubted, there'd be nothing in it for a freelance while just about every paper was rushing to the scene. On the other hand, I could get an exclusive here. I decided to stick it out.'

Detective Chief Inspector Ovenstone had listened to this exchange with increasing impatience. 'I've no intention of waiting around here at your beck and call,' he said. Keith tried to break in but Ovenstone raised his voice and ignored any attempt to interrupt. 'If there was a helicopter crash, I'd have heard of it.

'I've no reason to believe that there's any connection between the two cases. If you've any evidence to the contrary, I want it now.' He smiled, with maddening superiority. 'At first, we took your statement to my sergeant very seriously. Especially when we found an entry in Laurie's diary for the day he died. It said "D.Bruce, Rutherglen", and underneath was a word which might have been "guns". You won't know this, but Danny Bruce has been in prison—'

'He's a fence,' Keith said. 'And he lives in Rutherglen Gardens.'

'That's right,' Ovenstone said. 'What's more, Laurie spent the day he died in Glasgow, so he could not have been the dealer who came here. The entry in his diary read "Rutherglen g-d-n-s". So there's no connection.'

'The two cases are connected, all right,' Keith said. 'I'm not wholly sure how yet, but they are. I know it and I'll prove it to you before I'm done.'

'I'll say one thing for you,' Philip said admiringly. 'You've got grit!'

'Grit?' Keith said. 'Grit? That's it! I think you've just said the magic word.'

'You can sort all this out later,' the detective chief inspector said sharply. 'If you've got anything for me, I want it now.'

'Be patient,' Keith said. 'If you'll just give me a minute—'

'Not another moment! I can always arrest you for hampering the police and withholding information,' Ovenstone pointed out. He was a tall man and he drew himself up to seem taller, but he had a drooping moustache which Keith suspected was designed to hide a weak mouth.

'You probably could,' Keith said. 'In which case you'd get the story a few minutes earlier and you wouldn't get the proof at all. Something's going to happen and—'

'What's going to happen?' Ovenstone asked impatiently.

'Shut up!' Keith snapped. To his surprise, Ovenstone fell silent, gaping at him. Keith hurried on before the policeman could regain the initiative. 'The reporters

130

have been decoyed away, and a trap was set which was supposed to keep me out of it. There are visitors coming. Let's get these cars hidden. Over the grass and round the back of the shrubbery. Then, when we're out of sight, I tell you the whole story.'

'It won't do the lawn any good,' Philip said, 'and the marks may give the game away.'

'The lawn's already chewed up with reporters' cars,' Keith pointed out. 'Get going. Molly!'

'I think we'd better do as he suggests,' Fleet said. Ovenstone grunted.

Molly and Deborah were waiting in the hatchback. Keith spoke to his wife through the open driver's window. 'Do you have cameras with you?'

'Yes, of course.' Molly, a dedicated wildlife photographer, would as soon have travelled without her cameras as Keith without his guns.

'Follow the other cars,' Keith said. 'Hide this one and bring your cameras back. Hurry. Deb, stay with me.'

Deborah jumped out and Molly drove off on to the grass. Keith, in a fever of impatience, waited with his daughter at the end of the drive, ready at an instant's notice to dive into hiding, until the other four returned. While he waited, he stole a look at the inventory before slipping it into his pocket. 'I thought so,' he said aloud.

'This way,' Keith said. He led them round the back of the house, at first over the lawn and then through a small rose-garden. They stepped over low hedges, skirted a rockery bright with alpines and passed the double garage.

Keith, as he went, was looking up at the roof of the house. 'This has to be the place,' he said suddenly.

'Why does it have to be what place?' Ovenstone

131

asked. His tone had changed from arrogant to plaintive.

'Get under cover,' Keith said. 'They could be here at any moment.' Beyond what was evidently a rear extension from the drive, a vegetable garden was screened by a hedge of clematis. Flowering was over for the year and the clematis was an untidy tangle. He led the way round it. On the far side, a walled compostheap provided a dirty but not uncomfortable seat. 'Sit down and you'll be out of sight,' Keith said.

They were facing across a wide strip of grass, a flower border and the drive to the back door of the house some sixty yards away. The mass of berberis, bright with berries, led round the corner towards the front door.

'I've had just about enough of—' Ovenstone began.

'Not yet,' Keith said urgently. 'Let me check something first.' He listened, but there was no sound of a vehicle yet. He walked quickly across to the back door, looked behind the screen of berberis and came back again. 'Right enough,' he said.

'What is?' asked the detective chief inspector. 'Please,' he added.

Keith started to put him out of at least part of his misery. 'Mrs Winterton took me over the house yesterday,' he said. 'I was looking for clues to the whereabouts of Mr Winterton's collection of guns. His very valuable collection. There were radiators in every room, but I never saw a boiler for the central heating. One of Danny Bruce's men had just been round the house – I saw him returning – and there was grit on the floor and on the soap in the cloakroom.'

'A boiler room?' Molly said suddenly.

'Exactly. So I looked at the chimneys and spotted the

132

one with a taller, fatter pot. See it? There's a manhole behind those shrubs and a flight of steps, leading down to a door. That's where they'll be, under the coal. And I'll bet my chance of reaching Heaven that Danny Bruce is coming for them.'

'And I've got this, exclusive,' Philip said. 'Molly, my darling, I'll be your agent for any shots you get.'

Detective Chief Inspector Ovenstone was looking less and less happy. 'But if Duncan Laurie—'

'Hush,' Keith said. 'Listen. Keep heads down and radios quiet.'

Round the house came the sound of an approaching vehicle.

'Could be reporters coming back,' Keith said. 'But if it's not, it'll be a group of very hard men, probably armed. Let Molly photograph them removing the goods before you make any move towards arresting them. You want me to get a gun from my jeep?'

'Certainly not,' Ovenstone said. 'That's not how we operate in this country. You stay out of it. Fleet and I can cope. We've tackled armed men before.'

Detective Inspector Fleet was looking unhappy. 'This is my case,' he said, 'and if we have reason to believe that the men are armed—'

'That's only a guess,' Ovenstone said. 'We're told that the two cases are connected, and I have the rank. No guns. I know what I'm doing. We could use our driver, though.'

Keith could have pointed out that the man who was predicting guns was the man who said that the two cases were connected, but he decided to let Ovenstone have it both ways. Few things put his back up like a statement that the speaker knew what he was doing. In his experience, the contrary was usually true. 'I'll send him,' he said.

'Tell him to radio for reinforcements,' Fleet said.

A vehicle passed from tarmac on to gravel. The sound increased as a Range Rover came round the corner of the house. It halted when it had passed the end of the berberis. 'Debbie, you can come with me,' Keith whispered. 'Molly and Philip, you stay right here, out of sight, and for the love of God don't get involved.'

'What grounds do we have for an arrest?' Fleet whispered.

The men in the Range Rover were sitting still, using their eyes. There seemed to be four men and Mary Bruce. 'Don't move,' Keith whispered. 'They can't see us as long as you keep perfectly still. Grounds? I'm the executor for this estate. Anybody, anybody at all, removing anything from this house or its policies without my written permission is a thief. That'll do to be getting along with.'

The new arrivals seemed satisfied that they were alone. They began to disembark. Keith saw that Danny Bruce himself, immaculate as ever in camel-hair coat and trilby, was the first one out. Mary Bruce remained in the Range Rover. Her father took up sentry-duty at the corner of the house. The others descended the hidden steps, their heads seeming to sink as if they were walking into quicksand.

'Come, Deb,' Keith whispered. 'Keep low and don't make a sound, as if we were stalking rabbits.'

The vegetable garden had a slight upward slope away from the house so that an unseen retreat in that direction was out of the question. They crawled back in the direction from which they had arrived, their concealment aided by the grasses which had been

134

drawn up into the hedge, until they reached the double garage. A specimen weeping ash cut them off from Danny Bruce until they were behind the house.

As they hurried, now upright, through the garden, Keith was worried by Ovenstone's attitude and he was sure that Fleet was none too happy. There is a type of policeman, as there is a type of lollipop man, who believes that official status brings invulnerability, and the longer this delusion survives the stronger it can become. When Danny Bruce chose hard men he chose well, and Keith knew that he had been lucky to get on top of them and to stay there. They would not be overcome so easily a second time.

He decided to take Ovenstone's name in vain.

They passed Philip's minibus and the hatchback and found the police-car. All three were well tucked into the jungle but the police-car seemed to have a possible route forward on to the drive. The uniformed constable dozing behind the wheel jumped as Keith appeared at the window.

'Detective Chief Inspector Ovenstone says you're to pull forward and block the drive,' Keith said. 'Your engine's quieter than mine.' And if any car were going to be rammed he would prefer that it were the police BMW rather than either of his own cars. 'Then get on your radio and call for assistance. There are four men and a woman, probably armed. After that, you go and join your bosses, without showing yourself.' He described the covert route back to the vegetable garden.

They held branches back while the constable eased the car forward and parked it across the drive. He was a good driver and managed it without raising the engine's noise noticeably above tickover. While he was on his radio, Keith beckoned to Deborah and they faded

135

away. There was no sign of another sentry.

The jeep was as Keith had left it. He unlocked the back door. 'What did you make of Chief Inspector Ovenstone?' he asked Deborah.

'I thought . . . .' She paused and looked at him. 'I thought he was silly. You warned him, but he still thinks Danny Bruce and his men are going to give up just because he tells them they're under arrest.'

'I agree with every word,' Keith said. 'Well, it's on his own head if anything happens to him. I just hope your mother keeps her head down. The question is, what are we going to do, you and I?'

Deborah shrugged. 'You've already made up your mind,' she said.

'As a matter of fact, I haven't. Let's assume that, before reinforcements arrive, the Range Rover comes back down the drive. I don't think it can get past the police-car. What will they do?'

'Get out and run for it?' Deborah suggested.

'Very likely,' Keith said. 'And probably taking the most precious items with them. I don't much like that idea. They'll be caught, but just suppose they've hidden the pearls of the collection.'

'They could be all rusted by the time we got them back,' Deborah said.

'That's for sure,' Keith opened the back door of the jeep, lifted the rubber mat and unlocked a trap in the floor. This opened a narrow, specially-built compartment, squeezed between the exhaust and the fuel tank, where he kept a couple of guns and some ammunition. Old and inexpensive as they were, the guns were carefully wrapped. No unexpected invitation to shoot was going to catch Keith unprepared.

He handed Deborah the twenty-bore and a handful

of blue cartridges. 'Take this,' he said, 'but only if you're absolutely sure.'

'I'm sure,' she said. 'What do I do?'

'Back me up. Don't shoot unless somebody's coming at you or you think I'm in danger.'

'And—'

'Hush a minute,' he said. He thought quickly. Wherever the Range Rover stopped, there would be shrubbery close to the doors on either side. Better to allow them to emerge and to catch them nearer the gates. He placed Deborah behind a tree thirty yards beyond the police-car, and settled down in the bushes across the drive from her.

Nothing happened for what seemed an age.

'Dad, how long do we wait?' Deborah's voice came suddenly.

'Something will happen eventually,' Keith said. 'Until then, we hang on.'

Two minutes later they heard the Range Rover coming fast and his mouth went dry. Detective Chief Inspector Ovenstonc's belief that three unarmed policemen could arrest an armed gang had proved false. If Molly had disobeyed his last instruction . . . .

The Range Rover came round the curve of the drive, already over 50 m.p.h. and still accelerating. The driver must have been distracted by something in his mirror or within the vehicle, because he left his brakes off for a few more seconds. The drive had a dusting of old leaves and when he braked the big car began to slide. He let up, corrected and tried again but it was already too late. As a last resort he tried to crash through off the drive but the resilient bushes threw him back. He hit the bonnet of the police-car with a noise of crumpling metal and tinkling glass, followed by a moment of deathly silence.

Through the leaves, Keith saw an argument raging inside the vehicle. The Range Rover's engine had stalled. The driver tried his starter but it was a forlorn hope. Hideous noises made it clear that the vehicle was beyond moving under its own power.

There was more argument. Then a door opened and Danny Bruce's dapper backside emerged. '. . . to the road and grab the first vehicle to come along,' he was saying. 'Bring what you can carry.'

Keith waited until the motley group was almost abreast of them while he did a visual check of the guns on display. Musket . . . musket . . . pair of duellers . . . jezail and not a modern weapon to be seen. He stepped out of cover.

'Don't drop those guns,' he said. Even as he spoke, the words seemed odd. The order was intended to keep the treasures undamaged rather than the hands of the enemy full, but it served both purposes. 'Hold them over your heads. Anyone who doesn't is going to lose some bits.'

During the instant in which they were making up their minds, he put his safety-catch off with a vicious little snick. It was enough. Hands were raised.

'Even me?' Mary Bruce asked sweetly.

'Especially you,' Keith said.

Most of the group had been caught in the open but one man was close to the greenery. He made a sudden dive sideways and vanished. Keith stood fast, impressing his domination over the remainder. But, inside, he was praying. The man was heading towards Deborah. He prayed that she would either shoot or run. If she froze . . . .

The bushes parted again and the man backed

hurriedly out, still holding a miquelet. Keith recognised him by the dressing on his face and the blood pouring over his chin. Deborah followed, her muzzles centred on his chest. Her face was contorted into a snarl like that of a cat on the point of attack.

Keith felt again the crawl of atavistic dread up the back of his neck, but he kept his voice calm. 'Hullo, Nigel. Welcome back. I see you've bust your nose again. About turn, everyone, and start back. Squeeze between the cars. The first one even to look round gets shot where it'll do most harm. I'm not in a mood to take chances.'

'Do what he says,' Mary said. 'The bugger's mad.'

Danny Bruce, true to form, had the steel-and-silver, Scottish snaphaunce in his hands. 'He does seem to be a stumbling-block,' he said. 'One of these days . . .'

'Just walk,' Keith said. 'And if I find that any one's been badly damaged you're for it. Where's Eric?'

'Not feeling up to walking. Which is probably just as well. The way he feels,' Danny Bruce said thoughtfully, 'he wouldn't have stopped for a shotgun.'

'None of you had better feel the same,' Keith said, 'or blood will flow. No more talking or I'll think you're setting me up. And if one of those guns gets dropped I'll have to repair it. I'll harden the parts the old way, with bonemeal charcoal. And guess whose bones I'll use.'

He stole a glance at Deborah, but the alien creature had vanished. She grinned at him and winked. He blew out a long breath. So it had been an act. He had half-suspected some changeling . . . .

They plodded back towards the house with an interesting variety of limps. Keith dropped back a few paces. He winked back at Deborah. Tucking his own gun under one arm he took her gun from her, unloaded and closed it before handing it back. As they neared the end of the drive, he slid sideways into the bushes but continued on a parallel track, covering the party from there. It was folly, he knew. But Detective Chief Inspector Ovenstone had put his back most thoroughly up and, despite his anxiety, it tickled something deep inside him irresistibly to see the party marched back by a schoolgirl with an unloaded gun under the eye and camera of the nation's press. . . .

The scene which was appearing could not have been bettered. Molly had now emerged from hiding and was busily photographing the three policemen, who were handcuffed together. One of the pairs of handcuffs passed behind a stout downpipe. At first sight of the file of prisoners she poised for flight. Then she saw Deborah in command. The dedicated photographer united with the fond mother. She moved sideways to capture the whole scene, the automatic camera buzzing like a trapped insect.

Keith tucked his magnum twelve-bore behind his leg whence he could produce it in a hurry and came a few paces into the open. 'Down on your faces,' he said. 'Quickly. Philip, search them for guns, modern ones. Don't get in Deborah's way.'

'And get the handcuff keys out of the woman's handbag,' Fleet said.

The three officers were freed. Detective Inspector Fleet armed himself with a 9 mm. Luger from the collection. Ovenstone, black as thunder, rounded on Deborah. 'Give me that,' he said, grabbing the twenty-bore gun. 'You've no business to be waving shotguns around, at your age.'

'You're the one who's waving it around,' Deborah

140

pointed out. 'Anyway, it isn't loaded.'

Philip Stratton, who was scribbling rapidly in his note-book, snorted with laughter.

Molly had other things on her mind. 'Keith,' she said sharply. 'Don't do that.'

Keith looked up. He was sitting on the grass, his shotgun beside him. He had donned his cotton gloves and was gently wiping the coal-dust from the Scottish long gun with his handkerchief. 'I won't scratch it,' he said.

'I know you won't scratch it,' Molly said. 'I was thinking about your handkerchief.'

Keith muttered something rude about his handkerchief. He stopped work and held up his hand. 'Molly, what's this on my glove?'

Molly stooped. 'Coal-dust,' she said.

'Not that. On the side of my thumb.'

'A blonde hair,' Molly said. 'I could have betted on it.'

'You'd have lost.' Keith resumed his labour of love. 'You beauty,' he said. 'You little beauty.'

EIGHT

Even after the arrival of reinforcements, the period of delay and confusion which Keith had learned to expect after any police action was extended and exacerbated by the fact that the drive was blocked and by Keith's absolute refusal to have the Range Rover towed away until every gun from Robin Winterton's collection had been removed, checked, listed and transferred to a police van for temporary safekeeping by the police.

Philip Stratton had almost wrenched from Molly's camera the film which recorded the capture, at gunpoint, of the three officers and the similar capture of the culprits by her daughter. While he made intensive use of his radio-telephone, the Calders were left to stand around on the gravel or to wait in their cars. Keith ran out of patience. At least he could have made a start to checking the inventory. He boosted Deborah through a high window-opening and she opened the front door.

The mild panic which ensued when the Calders were found to have vanished only abated when Deborah and Molly were discovered, drinking tea in the drawing room. Keith, who was pacing around the house with a mug in one hand, the inventory in the other and a parcel under his arm, was persuaded to join them.

By common agreement between Detective Chief Inspector Ovenstone and Detective Inspector Fleet, a single constable to take notes was deemed sufficient. Even so, by the time that Philip Stratton had slipped unobtrusively into a corner, the available seating was filled. Ovenstone, still in surly mood after an unsuccessful attempt to persuade Philip Stratton not to market Molly's photographs, had taken one of the armchairs and Keith the other. Fleet, who was making a poor attempt to conceal his delight at Ovenstone's discomfiture, was squeezed on to the settee between Molly and Deborah and seemed to be enjoying the company.

'Now, see here . . . .' Ovenstone began.

'One moment,' Fleet said. 'You may have the rank, but we're on my patch and what we're going to discuss relates more to my case than to yours. I think I should have first crack.'

'Oh, very well.' Ovenstone almost managed to flounce in his chair and looked out of one of the long windows. The garden, beautiful under the declining sun, seemed to give him little comfort.

'In point of fact,' Keith said, 'the two cases are bound up closely together. I'll give you a written statement in due course, dotting the tees and crossing the eyes. Suppose I just hit the high spots for the moment? Then you can both ask questions.'

'That'll do fine,' Fleet said. Ovenstone grunted.

'And you can probably fill in some gaps,' Keith said. 'This is mostly the story of a very foolish old woman, who had been pampered all her life into such arrogance that she couldn't believe that she could possibly be

143

wrong about anything,' Keith said. 'You must know the type.'

'Know it?' Fleet said. 'I think I married its daughter. Sorry,' he added, in response to a disapproving glare from Ovenstone. 'Go on.'

'At one time or another, she dominated her son and her stepson – the sort of domination which can be achieved through the purse-strings, backed by a battering with words. It becomes a habit in the end. She tried with partial success to dominate her second husband. I suspect that it was her foolish indulgence which turned her son into a raving homosexual, but when she found out his . . . tendency, according to the former maid, she transferred her affection and her favours entirely to her stepson.

'Robin Winterton was concerned about this. He felt that Steven Clune was being unfairly treated and in the many family rows he sided with him. He might even have got around to mentioning him in his will, in the certain knowledge that he would get no benefit from his mother's inheritance, but there's no sign that he ever did anything about it.

'Robin Winterton was a sensible old chap. His only act of folly seems to have been his second marriage. Through his first wife he inherited some property, including some antique guns of very great value, and, realising that these were very much an appreciating asset, he extended the collection during the rest of his working life, as his form of life-savings.

'After I heard of his death, I took a look at the list I'd been keeping of his collection. I can't be sure, because he didn't buy everything through me, but I'd guess that he'd only spent around forty thousand.'

'Only?' Molly said.

144

'Think of it as an average of twenty quid a week out of the earnings of a successful career and you may see it in perspective. Those guns alone will fetch nearly half a million quid now. But add to them the almost priceless guns which came through his first wife and he could have been a millionaire, at least once.'

'Can't you be more specific?' Fleet asked. 'A court will need to know.'

'I have a rough figure in mind for what final disposal should realise,' Keith said, 'but I'm quite prepared to be astonished. You never know what collectors and museums will go to at auction when something unrepeatable turns up.

'The tragedy is that his family could not appreciate the wealth which he was accumulating. I'm not sure that he fully understood it himself. His will may have been very much out-of-date, or perhaps he meant it that way, but the hundred thousand each which he willed to his son and his daughter were a couple of drops in a biggish bucket. The balance, after capital transfer tax on the whole, was willed to his wife.

'As far as his family was concerned, he had been a salaried man with a pension which would die with him. He owned a fine house but lived modestly. He made no secret of the fact that his money was in a gun collection which his wife regarded as no more than an annoying hobby. She seems to have realised that it was valuable, but value is a relative term. The same applies to certain other antiques, mostly deriving from his first marriage.

'That's the background. Now we approach the facts.

'After Mr Winterton was murdered, his widow confessed that she had sold his collection, for far less than its value, to a knocker who had called at the door and who, from her description, seemed to have been

145

Duncan Laurie. Later, I was approached by Danny Bruce's daughter Mary.

'I knew the Bruces of old. I used to do business with them until I found that they were trying to unload stolen guns through me. Danny is an antique-dealer in Glasgow. Unless he's changed, he's also the premier fence for most of Scotland and northern England. And his intelligence system was always superlative – news from the worlds of crime or of antiques was part of his stock-in-trade. You probably know that as well as I do.

'Mary's approach to me was guarded. She was after information. Danny evidently had wind of the value of Mr Winterton's guns. But I couldn't make out whether Mary was sniffing after their whereabouts or their value to me as executor. Either Danny Bruce had staged the whole thing including the murder, or he had sent the knocker to buy them after he heard about Mr Winterton's death, or else he had had nothing to do with either event but had got wind that the guns were missing and was trying to get his hands on them anyway.

'I tried to cover all those possibilities.' Keith looked at Ovenstone. 'I told your sergeant about the guns. You didn't take it seriously because you learned that Laurie had been in Glasgow when he was supposed to have been visiting Mrs Winterton. That didn't matter a lot, because in fact Duncan Laurie never saw or, as far as I know, even heard of the guns. Yet he got drawn into the events.'

Ovenstone had been sitting in silence, but his reserve broke. 'I thought you said—'

'Wait,' Keith said. 'Please wait. I asked a friend in the Strathclyde police to keep an eye on Danny Bruce's movement of goods. And I set my brother-in-law to following Mary Bruce – I suppose I should call her

146

Mary Anguillas – who was travelling with a bodyguard of two toughs.

'Mary made a bee-line for Steven Clune. Her two goons tied him up and then they – with or without her assistance – beat hell out of him until he handed over ... this.' Keith picked up the plastic bag containing the handbag, from beside his chair. Four pairs of eyes followed it. 'I pinched it out of her car yesterday. Its purpose seems to have been blackmail and our best guess is that it's the handbag of the girl who was raped and murdered at Granton a few months ago, Jean Watson. I haven't opened the wrappings,' he added.

Chief Detective Inspector Ovenstone assumed the privilege of seniority and received the package. Without opening the polythene bag he managed to unlatch the handbag and to take a clouded look at the contents. 'Blue checked handkerchief and a green purse,' he said. 'That's all I can make out. We'll keep the whole parcel intact for the lab. But it's enough. It fits. Our colleagues will be turning handsprings.' Ovenstone himself was looking happier. The humiliating publicity of his capture by the Bruces and his rescue by a schoolgirl would be offset if he could bring in the solution to the Jean Watson case.

'Assume that Michael Winterton's fingerprints are on it, or that he thinks they are,' Keith said. 'After all, they could hardly be the widow's. That would be the hold which Steven Clune had over his stepbrother. And, Danny Bruce having the grip that he's got on the grape-vines of crime, he knew that some such incriminating evidence existed.

'The fact that he wanted it at all suggested very strongly that Danny-boy was only trying to cut himself a piece of the cake ... *post hoc*, as the lawyers would

147

say. This is confirmed up to the hilt if the description which Mary Bruce brought me of Mr Winterton's murderer was the truth – and, of course, if the murderer was still alive. Danny would never have pointed the finger at anyone who might have pointed it back.' He looked at Fleet and awaited a comment.

'A yes on both counts,' Fleet said. 'The description went to Records and fitted one man like a glove. A message reached me over the radio just before I came indoors. The police in Kirkcaldy picked him up. He still had the gold watch in his possession. The brass book-end was found in a dustbin two streets away. He's in process of coughing the lot at this moment.'

'You could have told me before now,' Keith said. 'It would have shortened the story. Anyway, it does confirm that Danny Bruce was a late arrival on the scene.

'It also suggests that the widow did tell the truth at least once, when she stated that she arrived home to find her husband dead.

'You thought that she might have killed him?' Molly asked.

'She didn't,' Inspector Fleet said. 'We had to consider her, of course. But Mr Winterton made several phone-calls while she was out. And she didn't have enough time between being dropped by her friend and the arrival of the police to clean herself up after – if the ladies will forgive me – so messy a killing.'

'I wondered about that,' Keith said. 'There was the possibility that Robin Winterton might have intended to change his will. She could easily have done it before she went out. No reputable pathologist will ever pinpoint the time of a death, not unless he saw the murder committed. There are too many variables and

148

his evidence is too easily upset by the thousands of cases in which precise estimates of the time of death have been proved to be hours or even days out. And I thought that Steven Clune might have killed his stepfather. But he picked up his mother after we conferred in the solicitor's office – by royal command, I suppose.

'If you arrive here by car, it's difficult not to park opposite the front door. And, just at the moment, not only are rowan berries falling there but the birds are dropping purple plonks from the trees – I think they've been eating the berberis berries. It makes a hell of a mess.'

'Doesn't it just!' Philip Stratton said.

'Clune's car had the dust of weeks on the roof,' Keith said, 'but no stains. When I saw Michael Winterton's car in Edinburgh, however, I leaned on the roof. It was freshly washed, but there were still one or two rowan berries in the gutter. And Duncan Laurie's van was all splattered with purple.'

'You just said that he never saw or heard of the guns,' Ovenstone said.

'He didn't.'

'But Michael Winterton didn't kill his father,' Molly said despairingly. 'We know that.'

'That's right,' Keith said. He turned to Detective Inspector Fleet. 'Mrs Winterton called the police, late on the Monday evening. How long were your team at the house?'

'We finished on Wednesday morning, sealed the two relevant rooms and left,' Fleet said.

'Was the widow in the house, and alone, all that time?'

'Several visitors came to offer help or condolences,'

Fleet said. 'Her stepson among them. So much for berries on his car.'

'Indeed, yes,' Keith said. 'Because she assured Mr Enterkin and myself that he hadn't looked near her. And she summoned her own son to chauffeur her although she usually used the local taxi. She was trying to foster the impression that she was still friends with her son rather than her stepson. And I'll tell you why. I'm speculating, but—'

'Go ahead and speculate,' Fleet said. 'Finding the evidence is our job.'

'Right. During those two days, Michael Winterton and his affectionate stepmother compared notes. Remember that he was very much under her thumb. As they saw it, in their inadequate understanding of his finances, Mr Winterton's assets would hardly cover the legacies to Michael and his sister; and he would certainly be blackmailed out of his share by his stepbrother. They couldn't bring themselves to believe that, after capital transfer tax on the whole was paid, there'd be anything much left for his widow. And this seemed very unfair to them.

'So, they thought, why not keep the gun collection separate? The value of this house and its contents might realise enough to pay perhaps half of the legacies to Michael and his sister. The value of the guns could remain unknown to Steven and to the Inland Revenue.

'As soon as the police left the house, Michael moved the guns out of their cellar and hid them under the coal in the boiler room. He must have been out of his mind.'

'With anxiety, you mean?' Molly asked. 'Or do you mean that he was mad to think that he could get away with it?'

'I was thinking of the damage he could have done to

150

what are really national treasures,' Keith said indignantly.

'On Thursday morning,' he went on, 'I returned from my wanderings. Mr Enterkin called a meeting that afternoon and the widow coolly announced that she had sold the guns. Well, she got a shock but she covered it well. I gave her some idea of the probable value of the guns.

'If she had had the sort of mind which could be changed, she could still have backed off. She could, for instance, have spun some tale about the guns still being nearby and awaiting collection and that she would cancel the deal. But no. The chance to cheat her stepdaughter, the tax man and her own son of even greater amounts still looked good.

'But I was pressing her for details of the sale and in her confusion she made a bad mistake. She had to describe a knocker and she described one who had called at the door earlier in the week. Duncan Laurie's visit must have been during Monday or it would have been noted by the officers in the house. I pressed her for more details. I asked whether there had been any packing-case in the van. She described the first case which came into her head, which happened to be an old and valuable dower chest. I've just been looking in the inventory. The dower chest is mentioned but I see no sign of it in the house.

'She had arranged for her son to transport her. This may have been because she and her stepson had decided to play down their closeness or because she wanted an opportunity to try and persuade Steven Clune to give up the evidence he was holding over his stepbrother. Whatever the reason, she capitalised on it by stating that her stepson hadn't been near her since

151

his father's death.

'There must have been another conference, probably by telephone, between her and Michael Winterton. I call it a conference, but more likely she was dispensing tablets of stone. It was decided to go through with the theft or embezzlement, whichever you like to call it. From Michael's viewpoint, the idea of getting access to a lot of money which neither his stepbrother nor anybody else knew about would have seemed attractive beyond his powers to resist. Remember, he would have been facing the possibility of becoming a fugitive if his other crime had surfaced.

'So far, it's almost a humdrum story of muddled thinking and bad intentions. Here's where it becomes truly evil.' He paused and wiped his face. The room seemed suddenly oppressive. 'The snag they faced was that Mrs Winterton had described a real man who would almost certainly be able to prove that he had nothing to do with the guns.'

Chief Detective Inspector Ovenstone had been recovering his humour. His flush had subsided and, no longer glaring out of the window, he had been listening attentively. 'You're suggesting that Duncan Laurie was killed for no better reason than to support a story which accounted for the disappearance of some valuable guns?'

Keith shrugged. 'Many men have been killed for less,' he said. 'May I ask why you decided that he hadn't killed himself?'

Ovenstone hesitated. 'I suppose there's no harm,' he said reluctantly. 'It seemed a clear case of suicide, but we had a pathologist look at him, just in case. The pathologist reported that the wounds had been made by a weapon much sharper than the razors – which seemed

152

to have been used for sharpening pencils and the like –
and with a shorter blade.'

'Like a veterinary scalpel?' Fleet asked.

'Could be. And the tentative cuts had been made
after death. A suicide by knife,' Ovenstone explained
kindly, 'usually makes some preliminary cuts before he
gets up the nerve to do the real job.' (Keith avoided
Molly's eye.) 'Do you really want your daughter
listening to all this?' Ovenstone asked suddenly.

'I think it would do her more harm to sit outside and
imagine things,' Molly said.

'And I was the one who caught the Bruce gang for
you,' Deborah said indignantly.

Ovenstone coloured again.

Keith hid a smile. 'The press will be all over her,' he
said, 'so she'd better know what not to say. You'll
feature as a beautiful blonde,' he added to Deborah,
'but don't let it go to your head. They called Smelly
Nelly a beautiful blonde when she had to be rescued
from a fire in that hovel of hers.'

Philip Stratton gave him a look of reproach. 'I
wouldn't count on it,' he told Deborah.

'Try this for size,' Keith resumed. 'Michael Winterton hurried over to Halleydane House as soon as he
could. Remember, he already had one murder to his
credit; the next would come easier.'

'If you're right,' Ovenstone said, '– and it's a big if –
he may have had more than one.' He glared at Philip.
'This isn't for publication until we release it. There
have been three other rape-murders in the Lothians
during the last five years which seem to show similar
features.'

'All the easier, then,' Keith said. 'And I suppose
that, in his line of work, he'd come to think less and less

153

about the sanctity of life.

'In that big estate-car of his he collected the dower chest and an old set of razors. He returned to Edinburgh and found Duncan Laurie's store. Probably he had on a boiler-suit and gloves. He offered to sell Laurie the set of razors and as Laurie sat at his table to look at them he took a scalpel out of his pocket and . . . did the deed. Then he carried in the dower chest.'

'If fits very well,' Ovenstone said slowly. 'All we need is evidence. Are the razors mentioned in the inventory?'

Keith had the inventory turned to the page. 'Very tersely,' he said. 'It just mentions razors, set, one, without any description. It could refer to the Rolls razor which Robin Winterton habitually used. But the dower chest is described, so they needed a replacement before the widow dared cough up the inventory – of which she thought she had the only copy. She tried the antique-dealers without success. But I found out, quite by chance, that Dougall and Symington, the cabinetmakers in Craiglockhart, are knocking up a dower chest as an urgent job for a cash customer who left a deposit instead of his name.'

'That could tie it up,' Ovenstone said.

'If he hasn't used an intermediary. When you start questioning the locals,' Keith said, 'you'll be looking for anyone who saw Michael Winterton or his car near Duncan Laurie's store on the Thursday night. Ask about Friday morning as well.'

'Why Friday morning?'

'After I found Laurie's body,' Keith said, 'I noticed the smell of his hair-oil on the fingers of my right hand. I had been careful not to touch the body at all. But I had shaken hands with Michael Winterton a few minutes earlier. I think that he'd realised that the lack of tentative cuts would make suicide less likely. So he went back in the morning – the murderer, true to form, revisiting the scene of the crime – and, seeing that the body hadn't been found, he went in and added them.'

Detective Inspector Fleet was still ruminating on his own half of the case. 'When you came to see me with the table-lighter, you implied that you thought that Mary Bruce's story was cock-and-bull.'

'Because that's what it was,' Keith said.

'Oh, come on,' Fleet said. He was sounding more human and less policemanlike by the minute. 'She seems to have been telling the absolute truth. Her description led us to the man Dunlap – keep that name under your hat too,' he added to Philip. 'So I can't help wondering whether Dunlap's visit to Danny's shop isn't what set him off on the trail of the guns.'

'It might have done if – what did you call him? – if Dunlap had ever been near Danny's shop,' Keith said. 'Danny knew who had killed Robin Winterton, simply because whispers go round in the criminal fraternity and they all get back to him in the end. Usually, such information would be as safe as in the confessional. Danny's reputation for care and confidentiality was his biggest asset, after Mary. This time, it suited Mary to divulge the real description, in the hope of sending me haring off again. But the table-lighter had nothing to do with it.'

'Dad,' Deborah said suddenly.

'Just a minute,' Fleet said. 'Your turn next. I don't understand.'

'Mary Bruce wasn't just dragging a red herring. She was also trying to explain away her presence here. If Dunlap had sold them anything from here, she'd have brought it with her. But she picked up the first expensive-looking ornament to come to hand. I was sitting where your constable is now, and the table-top was reflecting the light from the window. The maid had left a few days before, the daily woman had quit and Mrs Winterton wouldn't dream of doing her own dusting. There was a fine layer of dust on the table, but not where the lighter had been.'

'I see,' Fleet said. 'Well, there will be a thousand more questions. But . . .', he looked at Ovenstone, 'for the moment, we'd better be following up what we've already got.'

'I agree.'

'Dad,' Deborah said loudly. 'Where's Mrs Winterton?'

The two senior officers, who had been preparing to rise, subsided slowly.

'Mrs Winterton?' Keith said. 'What about Mrs Winterton?'

'Well, maybe I'm talking rubbish,' Deborah said bashfully, 'and if so stop me, but you're always telling us to see things through the other person's eyes and I think you've forgotten about Mrs Winterton, because I don't think you told her you'd pinched the evidence out of the boot of Mrs Anguillas' car.'

'No,' Keith said. 'I didn't. Maybe I should have told her.'

'I think you should, because Mrs Winterton came out and sent the reporters on a wild goose chase, so she must have been told to by Mr Bruce and why would she do what he told her if he didn't have anything to put pressure on her with?' Deborah finished, all on one breath.

'You mean that Mary Bruce wouldn't have known

156

that the evidence was gone until she got back to Glasgow?' Keith said. 'And then she'd guess that I'd taken it. She wouldn't tell Mrs Winterton that straight away. Just on the chance that Mrs Winterton mightn't know, she'd phone as if nothing had happened. Is that what you mean?'

'I think so,' Deborah said. 'I haven't thought it all out. I just wondered whether Mrs Winterton would go off on an ordinary visit just then, when she must have known that you were getting suspicious. I suppose she'd just done a deal with Mr Bruce.'

There was a hissing silence.

Keith turned to Philip Stratton. 'Did she put cases into the taxi?' he asked.

'Not that I noticed. But the reporters were scrambling into their cars and I was trying to persuade at least one or two of them and a photographer to stay behind. She could have done.'

'Bunked, by God!' Ovenstone said to Fleet. 'You phone the taxi firm, I'll use the radio in the car.' And, to the constable, 'You come with me.'

Keith caught Molly's eye and jerked his head. He gave Deborah the signal which he would have used to tell a dog to stay. She nodded back.

When Keith and Molly returned downstairs, Ovenstone was standing over Fleet, who was still at the phone. Both men looked up.

'I'd say that her best clothes have gone,' Molly said. 'She's done a flit.'

'Moir's taxi dropped her at the end of the Ring Road,' Fleet said, hanging up. 'She could have got another taxi. But there's been no sign of her at Turnhouse Airport.'

'There wouldn't be,' said Keith. 'Danny Bruce was

always in the market for stolen passports. I believe he usually had a hundred or more in stock. He could fit anybody, near enough, off-the-peg.'

'I don't like this at all,' Ovenstone said. 'Danny Bruce isn't the man to part with money before he'd got his hands on the goods. And yet he couldn't bilk her in case she squealed. But she wouldn't take off without the money. I've a nasty feeling we'll find her dead in a ditch.'

'That wouldn't be Danny's style at all,' Keith said. 'He prefers to be devious rather than violent. What he'd do would be to get her to do his dirty work, promise her money and get her to meet him. Then, and only then, he'd tell her that we'd got the incriminating handbag. Then she'd know the game was up. She'd have to go. He'd give her air tickets, passports and some money, with the promise of a cut sent out to Spain or Lichtenstein when he'd sold the guns.'

The driver came in from the car. 'The Dunbar police can't get any answer at the vet's surgery, sir,' he said.

'Gone, both of them,' Ovenstone snorted. 'I'll bet they were airborne before we got word to the airports.'

'She's made a jolly bad bargain,' Molly said. 'Think what she could have had and what she's left behind.'

'She hasn't left behind as much as she should have,' Keith said grimly.

It was after midnight before the Calders got to their beds. Keith was hardly asleep before Molly nudged him awake again. 'What did you do about Ronnie?' she asked.

Keith had quite forgotten about his brother-in-law, languishing in the cell behind some police-station. He grunted something unintelligible.

158

'Well, is he all right?'

'He's fine,' Keith said. 'Just fine.'

He went back to sleep.

Molly was on the phone to Wallace. 'Mrs Winterton and her stepson took the shuttle to Prestwick,' she said, 'and then flew to Barcelona. After that, they vanished.'

'Sounds like the right thing to do,' Wallace said.

'Keith's sick as mud, because she took a lot of valuable stuff away with her, including a Minton vase, which he's getting very uptight about, and some jade. He says he'll follow them to the ends of the earth and bring them back to justice. Can you talk some sense into him?'

'You can t-talk him out of it,' Wallace said. 'Point out that he can meet the legacies to Steven Clune and his sister from the price of the house and contents plus selling the less important parts of the collection. If he fetches Mrs Winterton and Michael ditto back to face t-trial, and they get off – which is always on the cards, juries being what they are – he'll have to sell the rest of the guns and hand over the money. As things stand at the moment, he can hang on to most of the collection, play with it and gloat over it, for years.'

Molly found her husband at his workbench on the upper floor of Briesland House. Here, two rooms had been devoted to his workshop and also housed the firm's stock of antique guns. The weather had broken again and the view to the town was obscured by rain. He preferred to look at the wall above his bench, where the two Scottish long guns were now mounted. A sixteen-bore sidelock lay dismantled on the bench.

Keith took the advice philosophically. He had already seen the point for himself. He told Molly that

159

Mrs Winterton could stay where she was and rot for all he cared.

'That's all right, then,' Molly said. 'Why do you want to hang on to them anyway? I thought you wanted your commission.'

'I do. But that'll go up as values rise. We've got a good little museum in the town,' Keith said dreamily. 'What I'd really like to do is to lay on a really good exhibition of gun-history, showing a good example of each style and associating them with historical events. That'd fetch the gun-buffs along. And then we could have a discreet poster advertising our stock . . . .'

Molly lowered herself into the worn old armchair. 'I can always tell when something's bothering you,' she said. 'You don't think it's all over. Do you?'

Keith swivelled round on his working stool. 'I don't think we know all the answers,' he said. 'But we may never know them all. In that sense, it probably is all over as far as we're concerned.'

'What answers don't we have?'

'There's a connection missing somewhere. It's all very well saying "Danny Bruce knew this" and "Danny Bruce knew that", but he knew a little too much too quickly. The value of the collection, the fact that I was the executor, that it had gone missing, that Steven Clune was blackmailing his stepbrother. Nobody's grape-vine's that good. And he didn't have time to find out all those things for himself. Somebody was feeding him with information.'

'Well, don't look at me,' Molly said. 'What did you hide in your drawer as I came in?'

'Nothing,' Keith said indignantly.

Molly jerked open the drawer. 'Oh, Keith!' she said. 'You haven't got time to build yourself a copy just now.

160

Guns are arriving for overhaul. They're wanted for the start of the season. It's not long off.'

'They should have been put in months ago,' Keith said. He grinned at her suddenly. 'Can you imagine the stir there'll be when I produce a perfect facsimile of a Scottish snaphaunce to shoot clay pigeons with?'

'I can imagine the stir there'll be if the Twelfth goes by and you haven't got on with those overhauls,' Molly said.

'I'll do them, I'll do them,' Keith said. He picked up a turnscrew. 'Slave-driver!'

'But,' Molly said, 'Steven Clune phoned. He says that there are some of his personal effects still stored at Halleydane House and he'd like to collect them. I said you'd meet him there in an hour's time.'

Keith looked out of the window. 'I don't want to go out in that.'

'Nonsense,' Molly said. 'The drive will do you good. Take Deborah with you.'

Keith put his turnscrew back in the rack.

NINE

There was no sign of Steven Clune's car when Keith rolled the jeep up to the front door of Halleydane House. The rain had stopped and a watery sun was trying to break through the heavy clouds, but the trees dripped and there were puddles on the gravel. The house seemed to know that it was no longer a home.

'I think you'd better go for a walk,' Keith told Deborah. 'Try not to get your feet wet or your mother'll blame me.'

'Oh, Dad!'

'Look, our slightly peculiar friend wants to uplift some of his personal effects. God knows what that mayn't include. You're better out of it.'

Deborah sighed gustily. 'All right,' she said. 'But sometimes you can be a real drag, you know that?'

'So your mother always tells me.' She put her tongue out at him and he retorted in kind. He unlocked the front door. When he looked round, she was out of sight.

It might be no part of an executor's duties to safeguard the assets of the estate, but Keith was conscientious. The first frosts could be expected soon, the house might stand empty all winter before being sold and once the shooting season was in full swing he might not think of it again. It took him some time to find the various stopcocks and drain down the systems, but he was flushing the last toilet before he heard Clune's voice calling him from the hall.

Clune, who was understandably subdued, had brought two empty suitcases. His chattels had been stored in a wardrobe in what had once been his room. They were obviously personal, the innocuous souvenirs of his boyhood, and Keith made no objection when he began to pack them.

The job was almost finished when Clune turned and sat down on the bed. He looked round at the muted décor. 'This room used to have such a bright paper,' he said. 'I don't remember what it showed. Toys, I think.'

Keith could think of no reply but an interrogatory noise.

'You despise me, don't you?' Clune said. 'I don't blame you. I despise myself. Not because I'm gay, although, coming back here and remembering, I can't help wondering what my life could have been like.'

'There's never any point looking back,' Keith said gruffly. He tried and failed to think of a topic to turn the subject.

'There's certainly nothing to look forward to,' Clune said desolately. 'My friend's walked out on me. He'd looked up to me until he saw what those men reduced me to. I'm nearly broke and my only source of extra income is out of the country. In fact, once they run out of funds he'll probably be writing to me for money. There's a laugh! And it's my fault. I'm the one who blew it.'

163

Keith was almost wriggling with embarrassment. 'Should you be telling me all this?'

'It helps to tell somebody. And there's nobody else now.'

'A trouble shared,' Keith said, 'is a trouble doubled.'

Clune ignored the hint. 'You were kind, that time when you found me. You and that girl of yours. She's a charmer.' Clune, who had been looking down and picking at the coverlet, suddenly looked up at Keith with almost doglike dependence. 'I've no other friends left. But at least I'm not going to be prosecuted. The police didn't have enough evidence about blackmail. And the Fiscal's office said that the chain of evidence connecting me with the . . . other thing was too broken. And they'll need my co-operation, if Michael ever comes to trial.'

Once started, Steven Clune seemed unable to stop himself. 'It wasn't so awful, what I did, was it? We'd been out for a meal together, Michael and I. We got on quite well, outside the family, despite our difference. Perhaps the fact that we both had that awful old woman to contend with gave us something in common. You needn't look at me like that. It may not be how you expect a man to talk about his mother, but we can't all choose our parents. You can't imagine what she was like to her family. Sweetly cloying one minute, over-bearing the next, very demanding and absolutely determined to get her own way.

'Michael had had a skinful that night, when it all started. I don't drink much, and anyway I was driving. The car was parked near the harbour. He said he wanted a pee and wandered off where it was dark. He didn't come back, but I wasn't bothered. I was sleepy and there was a superb performance of *La Traviata* on

164

the car radio.

'When it finished, I realised that he'd been gone an age and I went looking for him. It was black as the pit, so I started the car. The headlights caught him. I was just in time to see him roll her body off the sea-wall. There was never any doubt in my mind that she was dead. Nor about what he'd done to her first. There's a streak of ruthlessness in Michael, especially in his dealings with women. I suppose some things take us all different ways.

'The place was absolutely deserted. I got out and took his arm and started to lead him back towards the car, wondering what the hell to do. I knew what the law said I should do, I just didn't know what I was going to do. To look at it one way, I had the power to change certain things but not the things which needed to be changed. Do you see what I mean?'

'I think so,' Keith said. 'You could change your stepbrother's life but you couldn't bring the girl back.'

'I knew you'd understand. Then I saw that he had the girl's bag in his hands. I said something about it and he turned and threw it back towards where she'd gone over, but it didn't reach the water. I left him standing and swaying and I walked back for it. I was wearing gloves. On an impulse, I tucked it under my arm. He never noticed, he was too pissed.

'I got him back to the car and dropped the bag on the floor at the back. He started talking, babbling compulsively, the way I'm doing now. He said . . . he said that she was a tart, that she'd agreed to do it for ten quid, but that he was taking his time and she got impatient and that all he meant to do was to hold her down while he finished. He said he didn't mean to kill her. That's what he said, and I believed him.

'I can't say I was shocked. There have been times I've wanted to do terrible things to women. I've sometimes thought that there were too many of them in the world. Not recently, but earlier, when they shocked me.

'So I delivered him to his home and wrapped the bag in polythene to preserve any fingerprints. And I used it later to get a few quid out of him. After all, he could always get money out of her, and she was my mother not his. That was fair, wasn't it? Surely that was only fair.'

Keith had felt a great unease in his guts as the tale went on. He had wanted to protest, but now he found that he had nothing to say. If the police were right and Michael Winterton had been responsible for other sex-crimes, they would soon prove it. Time enough then for Steven Clune to learn that his stepbrother had been worse than he had painted himself.

'I'm not qualified to judge,' Keith said. He walked to the door. 'Come on. Finish the job and we'll get away from here.'

'Too many memories,' Clune said in agreement. He returned to his packing, but after a moment he looked up again. 'You've got a fine daughter there,' he said shyly. 'She's going to be a very caring sort of person, later. If I'd met somebody like her when I was younger, my life might have been very different. The reason that I was late was that she came and sat in the car with me.' Keith made a sudden movement. 'I didn't lay a finger on her,' Clune said quickly. 'You know I wouldn't. Too afraid of rejection, if for no other reason. We talked. I can't even remember what she said. But she was simple and natural and I began to see how a relationship between a man and a woman was possible. I didn't feel

166

lust, but I knew that I could have done. Do you understand?'

'I understand,' Keith said. 'I don't approve, but I understand.'

The cases were heavy – many of Clune's relics were books, the lighter classics of boyhood, retained for nostalgic rather than literary interest. Keith took one case and, after a last, backward look, Clune followed with the other.

Keith moved quickly. He was almost sure that Clune's words could be taken at face value, but he would be uneasy until he had seen that Deborah was unharmed. The talk of rape and murder had unsettled him. Such happenings might be rare, but he had been reminded that they did happen. The two men were stepbrothers and no kind of blood relations, but the common element in their background might have produced similarities in their aberrations.

At the bottom of the stairs, Clune stopped and Keith was forced to wait for him. 'That's it, then,' Clune said. 'I don't suppose I'll ever come here again.'

'That's for sure,' said a voice. The man Keith knew as Eric came out of the drawing-room door. He had a gun in his right hand. It had once been a hammerless shotgun, but was now sawn off at both ends.

Keith's first impulse was to throw the suitcase, but the intuition which is born of experience told him that such a weight could not be thrown quickly. With that weapon, Eric could blow his head off before the case was properly on its way. He put it down slowly.

'Sit down, both of you,' Eric said. Steven Clune moved towards the chair by the telephone. 'No, not there. On the floor, with your backs to the wall. But

167

first, you—', he pointed the gun at Keith who felt his chest contract, 'open your coat and turn around.' Keith did as he was told. 'Take the knife out of its sheath with your left hand, slowly, and drop it on the floor.' Again, Keith had no choice but to obey. 'So you're not carrying my revolver,' Eric said. His air of superior amusement had returned but with an added edge. 'Well, you never liked it anyway. You think this is better?'

'I could have got you a thousand quid for that before you went and sawed it off,' Keith said. His voice sounded hoarse.

'It didn't cost me anything.' Eric surveyed the seated pair with satisfaction. 'Isn't this nice! The two men I most wanted, and I catch you together. I was following you.' He nodded at Clune. 'I lost you at Lasswade, so I tried here on the off-chance and struck lucky.'

'You've already beaten me up once,' Clune wailed. 'What do you want now? What am I supposed to have done?'

Eric smiled unpleasantly. 'You don't know my name? Either of you?'

'You're Eric,' Keith said. 'That's what Mary called you.'

'I'm Eric Dunlap. Does that start any bells ringing?'

It meant something to Keith but, before he could speak, Steven Clune said, 'Dunlap? You're not Bobby's . . .?'

'Brother,' Eric said. 'I'm the big brother of your latest boy-friend.'

'It's over now,' Clune said drearily. 'You needn't worry. He's left me.'

'I took him away. But not before you'd debauched him, turned him into a half-and-half like yourself.

168

That's what the beating was for. I couldn't kill you just then. Not with the others looking on. Mary doesn't mind a little rough stuff but she doesn't go for snuffing. So I had to defer the pleasure for another time. Like now.'

'I didn't make him into anything he wasn't already,' Clune said. Keith thought that that was probably the wrong thing to say. And Clune's voice was quavering with fear. Keith could look for little help from that quarter.

Despite the seriousness of his predicament, a detached part of Keith's mind could feel the satisfaction of a mystery neatly resolved. One brother the lover of Steven Clune, one in Danny Bruce's employ. A third Dunlap – another brother? – tipped off that Halleydane House contained valuables and that the maid had left, watching the house and, seeing the taxi, thinking that both occupants had gone out. Danny Bruce's omniscience was explained.

Keith's complacence was short-lived. Eric called Clune an arse-bandit and then switched his attention. 'As for you, Calder,' he said, 'I'd been looking forward to this since Saturday. You made me look stupid in front of Mary, taking Nigel's shooter off me like that. And what you did . . . nobody does that to me and gets away with it.'

'I wasn't going to do you any real harm,' Keith said. 'You pushed a gun at me. And then Nigel, rushing at me—'

Seated as he was, with his back literally to the wall, there was no way that Keith could get up in a hurry. His knife was on the floor, only a yard away but out of reach. How long would it be before Deborah came to look for him? And did he even want her to come? She might be killed. But if she didn't come until too late . . . .

'Nigel's coming wouldn't've mattered if you hadn't already grabbed me exactly where I'm going to put a load of BB into you,' Eric said loudly. He was visibly working himself up into a passion. 'And now . . . Mary! She's going to go down for carrying concealed weapons and assaulting the police, and it's all down to you.'

Eric was standing with his back to the open front door. Keith saw the slim figure poised on the threshold and knew that he must hold the man's attention at all costs. 'If she'd asked me,' he said loudly, 'I'd have warned her not to pull a gun on those three coppers.'

Steven Clune had also seen it and from somewhere he produced a buried reserve of courage. 'Don't tell me that you're carrying a torch for that . . . that virago,' he said.

Deborah had vanished. How much had she seen and heard? Keith remembered that the jeep's keys were still in the car, with the key to the gun-locker attached. One of his fears had always been that she would be drawn into one of his scrapes and end up with a man's blood on her hands. He could not think what to hope for.

'If it's any of your business . . .' Eric began. He broke off. 'What did you call her?'

'It means a *femme fatale*,' Keith said quickly. 'A heart-breaker.'

'She's all of that. And now God knows when I'll see her again. Christ, how I'm going to enjoy this!' He lifted the gun, two-handed.

'You won't, you know,' Clune said. 'Revenge is never as sweet as you expect it to be. And Mary won't approve.'

170

'She won't know, ever. But I'll still have done it for her.'

Keith kept his voice calm and reasonable. 'I suppose Danny Bruce knew about the collection through Bobby and you?'

Eric scowled at him but at least he postponed pulling the triggers. 'If it matters, yes.'

'And the Dunlap who's been lifted for Robin Winterton's murder?'

'Our brother,' Eric said. 'But he always was a bloody fool. Mary told him to be sure that the house was empty. That's enough talking. You've got ten seconds to say your prayers.'

Keith's next gambit was dangerous but he could think of nothing else to say which might postpone a little longer what seemed to be becoming inevitable. 'Did you know that it was Mary who provided his description?'

'Balls!'

Keith hurried the discussion away from the unfortunate word. 'It's true,' he said. 'Just after we had our fight. You weren't in the room, but Nigel could have told you. She didn't name any names, but she described a man she said had sold something from here in one of her father's shops. I repeated that description to the police – not knowing, of course, that the man was any relative of yours. . . .' His tone sought to imply that if he had known that the man was Eric's brother he would have kept silence.

The sun had managed to break through. Outside the door, Keith could see the shadow of the rowans. A rowan tree to the north of a house is supposed to keep witches away. A pity – he could have used the services of a well-disposed witch. As the thought came to him, he

171

saw Deborah's figure reappear, his heavy magnum over her arm. Her face shone white.

Eric found his voice. 'That can't be true,' he said. 'Or else . . . maybe she didn't know his name.'

'She knew it, all right,' Keith said. 'She was prepared to see your brother taken up for murder, just to divert my attention while she made her play for the guns. Just . . . to . . . divert . . . attention,' he repeated loudly.

'Damn you, she wouldn't do that,' Eric yelled. He levelled his gun.

Deborah had taken the message and had moved to the side until she could no longer see Eric. She was out of Keith's view and when she fired he was sure for a moment that Eric had killed him.

Her shot swept a chiming clock off the wall and scattered it in fragments up the stairs.

As Eric swung round, Steven Clune moved with a speed and courage which astonished Keith. He was up, sweeping Keith's knife off the floor and sailing towards Eric in a flying tackle before Keith had half risen. Eric swung back and Keith ducked under the arc of the gun and flung himself flat. If Eric was, as he had said, using BB shot, even the fringe of the pattern would inflict appalling damage.

The second shot, fired within the confining walls, was deafening. The room was filled with the reek of burned nitrocellulose.

When Keith raised his head, he saw that both the other men were down. Eric had subsided against the wall beside the door, with the handle of Keith's knife protruding from the middle of his chest. Steven Clune had been flung on his back, his chest ripped open by the shot. Half the room was spattered red.

'Go back and wait at the car,' he called to Deborah.

172

Her white face peered in. 'Did I do it right?' she asked in a quavering voice.

'You were wonderful. Now go.'

Eric seemed dead but Keith kicked the gun beyond his reach, just in case. Steven Clune was still breathing, somehow, although one lung must have been collapsed. Heedless of the blood, Keith knelt down and cradled his head.

Clune managed to show his uneven teeth in a half-smile. Keith guessed that he was feeling little pain, saved by the numbness which often follows shock. 'Did I get him?' he whispered.

'Dead centre,' Keith said.

'That's good. And now I'm bleeding all over another carpet. Don't know what Mother would have said.' His whisper was getting very faint. 'Couldn't let that girl of yours . . . oh damn! Things might – I might – have been so different . . . if I'd ever known . . . a girl like that.'

He died without saying any more.